SMOKE IN THE VALLEY

Things had always been pretty peaceful in Trinity Valley, but with the formation of the Cattlemen's Association, trouble was not long in coming. The settlers felt they needed some protection against the big landowners, who wanted them out of the way. Then the lead began to fly. Now, from Tombstone, came the famous gunfighter, John Harding, whose skills were soon put to good use. Even so, there would be many candidates for Boot Hill before peace came to the range.

WES OVERLAND

SMOKE IN THE VALLEY

Complete and Unabridged

LINFORD
Leicester

First hardcover edition published in Great Britain
in 2003 by Robert Hale Limited, London

Originally published in paperback as
Smoke in the Valley by V. Joseph Hanson

First Linford Edition
published 2004, by arrangement with
Robert Hale Limited, London

British Library CIP Data

Overland, Wes
    Smoke in the valley.—Large print ed.—
Linford western library
1. Western stories
2. Large type books
I. Title II. Hanson, Vic J.
823.9′14 [F]

ISBN 1–84395–301–3

Published by
F. A. Thorpe (Publishing)
Anstey, Leicestershire

Set by Words & Graphics Ltd.
Anstey, Leicestershire
Printed and bound in Great Britain by
T. J. International Ltd., Padstow, Cornwall

This book is printed on acid-free paper

1

The red-haired youth leapt from the stagecoach, and he was running as soon as his heels hit the boardwalk. He ran for a few hundred yards, turned sharply and burst through the doors of the press-shop. In the dusky interior he skidded to a halt, panting.

In the left-hand corner of the shop a low-hanging lamp shed a sickly orange radiance on the old man bent over the type-rack. The youth's heels went clackety-clack on the boards as he advanced.

The old man finished his line and placed his setting stick carefully beside him. Then he looked up. His face was seamed in friendly lines; there were grin-wrinkles at the corners of the bright blue eyes. He was clean-shaven and his spare grey hair was brushed across his forehead in a smart little quif.

'What's bitin' you, Sam?' he said.

Sam Garner whipped a hand from his side, held out a long envelope, waved it a little. 'Despatch, Mr Mowbree — right from Tombstone.' His voice was high with excitement.

'Right from Tombstone, uh. D'yuh know what it's about, Sam?'

'Yes, suh. It's — '

The old man lifted an inkstained hand and his lips quirked into a smile. 'Don't tell me.'

He tore the envelope with a long thumbnail, extracted the paper and unfolded it.

As he read the message his face sobered. Businesslike and to the point:

John Harding had gun-fight in International Saloon. Killed two men. Unhurt himself. Sheriff arrested him. Let him go following morning. Self-defence.

BRODIE. Tombstone.

'It's about John Harding, ain't it, Mr Mowbree?' said Sam. 'I heard about it in Tombstone. Jasper never stops long — scared I guess. But I went in the saloon. I saw where he done it. When Mr Brodie gave me the despatch I guessed what it was about.'

'I told you never to go in that saloon.'

'I was only in there for a minute, Mr Mowbree. I didn't have nothin' to drink. Honest. Are we gonna have a special edition?'

'Special edition? What for? This ain't Tombstone.'

'Maybe John Harding 'ull come here.'

'I hope to God he don't.' The old man spoke half to himself. 'We've got enough trouble already.'

He turned with deliberate abruptness back to his work. He flung words over his shoulder.

'We'll give it a column. I'll set it up when I've finished this job. This is important. Get the press runnin', Sam.'

'Yes, sir.' Sam crossed the room. He

lit the hanging lantern over the long, battered press in the corner. 'Where's Sally, Mr Mowbree?'

'She's gone down to Mrs Murphy's to take them bills.'

'A few folks I could mention are gonna be hoppin' mad when they see them bills tacked up.'

The old man merely grunted. Sam shrugged and started the press; its thunder and clatter made further conversation impossible. The big machine was beside the plate-glass window which was boarded up at the bottom. Looking over the boards as he fed the sheets into the press, Sam could see what went on in the street outside.

A man, half-running, clattered by on the boardwalk. Somewhere out of Sam's sight another man shouted. Sam craned his neck. He could see nothing now but the dusty, rutted street, and a nag dozing at a tie-rail opposite.

He straightened a crumpled sheet. Then he jerked his head up once more. Boot-heels clattered. The man went by again, moving in the other direction. Another man followed him, dark, black-hatted Clay Hosell. The sheriff.

Sam turned his head the other way and looked at John Mowbree. The old man was intent at his work: he did not seem to have noticed anything. Boot-heels clattered again, the print-shop door was thrown open. With a quick motion Sam Garner stopped his machine.

Luke Sands burst in. He was a beanpole with an unruly thatch of yellow hair and a twist to his right foot which made his body jerk forward rhythmically as he walked in long strides. He did not stop striding until he was almost on top of John Mowbree and the old man's eyes were blazing quizzically up at him.

'John — Sol Murphy's bin slugged an' the bills taken off him . . . '

The old man's eyes widened. 'Have yuh seen Sally, Luke?'

'Nope . . . The sheriff's down there . . . '

Mowbree threw off his white apron,

shrugged into his black coat.

'Sam,' he said. 'You'd better come too. Lock up the place.'

'Yes, sir.'

He had to run to catch up with the two men. John Mowbree travelled at a shuffling run to keep up with Luke's long loppy strides. They were turning into the alley, together with folks coming from all sides, when the youth caught up with them.

The alley ran alongside the feed barn and was a short cut from the back-street. At the other end of it a knot of men gathered. Sheriff Clay Hosell, who was almost as tall as Luke Sands, towered above. He was shouting at them to get back — give room.

The two men and the youth reached the throng and Luke elbowed a way to the front for them. Doc Billings was bending over the bulk of Sol Murphy. Sol's face was covered in blood. He was beginning to stir, the whites of his eyes showed.

The sheriff was reading a dirty

crumpled handbill and frowning. He turned and saw John Mowbree and he said: 'Did you print this?' He struck at the bill with a long thick forefinger.

'Yes, I did, Clay.'

'I told yuh I didn't hold with this so-called Cattlemens' Association. It's causin' bad feelin'. This man might've been killed.'

'There ain't no law says we can't start an association an' print bills to advertise it.'

'Looks like somebody don't like your advertisement. This is the only one they left.' The sheriff waved it. He looked at Mowbree again and his dark eyes were a little kindlier.

'I'm sorry about this. Nobody saw what happened. Somebody must've slugged Sol as soon as he came around the corner. Jenky was in back o' the feed-barn when he heard the scuffle an' the bump. By the time he got round here all he found was Sol.'

'That's right,' said Jenky, a toothless old-timer.

'Just a scalp wound,' said Doc Billings. 'His skull's as hard as iron.'

Sol Murphy made a sound that was half groan, half growl. His eyes opened and rolled and he began to lever himself upwards. Doc put his arm around the bulky shoulders. Sol glared at him. Then he said: 'Oh, the sawbones! What hit me?'

'*Somebody* hit you!'

'That's what I'm thinkin'. Who was it?'

'Wal, if you don't know nobody else does,' said Clay Hosell.

'Oh, the sheriff's here too, is he?' Sol thrust aside the doctor's arm and rose. He swayed, but the set of his shoulders, the spray of his arms, kept everybody at a distance. Sol was Irish — and very independent.

He looked at Mowbree. 'They took me papers, John,' he said.

'We'll print more.' John Mowbree glanced at the sheriff, his blue eyes almost merry. The sheriff flushed a little but there was a half-smile on his lean dark face.

'We will that,' said Sol truculently. He gazed at the ring of faces. 'Didn't nobody see anythin'?'

'Nobody ain't come forward to say they did,' said the sheriff. He looked around him too, with none of Sol's truculence, but relaxed, mocking. The crowd shifted uncertainly.

'Come up to my place, Sol,' said Doc Billings. 'Let me fix that head.'

Sol wiped blood from his face with his sleeve, then he spat. He started forward suddenly as if the crowd were not there. They parted to let him through. He grinned as he passed John Mowbree. There was a hint of devilment in the old printer's smile, and in his twinkling blue eyes. Then the look became one of anxiety. He started forward after Sol, Sam Garner in his wake.

'Sol! Where's Sally?'

The Irishman turned his head as the pair caught up with him.

'She was with Ma when I left.'

'I wondered. I'll go there.'

'I'll be comin' for some more bills tonight.'

'They'll be ready.'

Sol went on with the doctor. Old John and young Sam turned back, skirted the bunch of rubbernecks and made for Ma Murphy's.

They had not gone far when they saw Sally coming towards them. She wore her blue jeans and yellow linen shirtwaist. She had a short Scotch plaid coat around her shoulders, and this blew a little in the breeze as she swung along. She wore high-heeled riding-boots which made her roll a little, her hips swaying. She had a shape to set any man's heart a-thumping, but nothing blowzy about it; she was as lithe and springy as a mountain-cat.

John Mowbree made a little clucking noise with his tongue: she had gone out wearing her hat but now, as usual, it was swinging from her shoulders by the lanyard and her rich goldy-brown hair was blowing in the breeze. It was like a cloud around her brown piquant face with the blue eyes like her father's: but much bigger, more like her mother's had been.

Seeing her like that gave John a queer clutch at his heart. He knew men, and he knew their thoughts. He knew all of them did not think of a lovely woman the way he did, and were not prepared to show her the same old-world courtesy. He clucked with his tongue as he saw Sally, her hands in her pockets like a boy — yet withal a vision of womanly loveliness to make a hard-boiled cowboy turn his head with the old wolf-light in his eyes and, who knows, the old wolf-call on his lips.

'Hallo, Dad — Sam,' she said.

They acknowledged her greeting. 'What kept you?' said her father.

'Why, what's the matter?' she said. Her voice was a little husky, a little breathless, as if laughter bubbled beneath it all the time. She did not wait for John's reply but went on: 'I met

Brad Simmons outside Mrs Murphy's. We stopped and talked a while.'

'You met Brad Simmons did you? Outside Mrs Murphy's — an' you talked to him there right in front of everybody. You know I don't like that young hellion, Sally — you know he's one of the Association's worst enemies . . .'

'You and your old Association! Brad can't help it if he belongs to a party which is against it, can he? He has a job to do just the same as you.'

'He pumped you I guess — tried to get to know all about things — '

'He did nothing of the kind.'

While they were talking the man and the youth had turned about. The girl fell into step with them, giving a little flounce of her hips as she spoke her last sentence.

John Mowbree said, with deceptive mildness, 'Sol's been slugged and his papers snatched. Not a single one left. Mebbe that's why Mr Brad Simmons kept you talking — so you wouldn't catch up with Sol an' get' in the way o' things.'

A little jerk of her head, a sharp intake of breath, revealed the impact the news had on the girl. There was silence for a few pregnant moments. Then, with the breathlessness of her husky voice more pronounced than ever, she said: 'Is — is Sol hurt badly?'

'It'd take more than a couple of those side-winding skunks to knock chips off a Murphy.' There was sudden laughter in the old man's voice and it was very like his daughter's.

'Where . . . ?'

'He was goin' up the alley side o' the feed-barn. He didn't see who hit him. What he's worried about is losing the papers.'

'He's tacked some up near his home. I saw them.'

'That's small consolation,' said the old man. He stopped talking, obviously waiting for his daughter to speak again.

She said breathlessly: 'Dad — I don't believe Brad Simmons stopped me just for that purpose. He's not that sly. He's — '

She seemed to grope for words and John said: 'You always come home through the alley, don't you?'

'Well — yes — usually.'

'An' Brad Simmons sees enough of you to know that, durn his hide. What did he stop you for? What did you talk about? Come on, Sally, better to tell me all about it instead o' the sheriff.'

'Oh, Dad, you wouldn't.'

The girl's speech was breathless and jerky. She kept stopping as if at loss for words. This fact did not escape the old man. He said: 'If Sol hadn't got such a hard head he might've been killed. Whether the sheriff's in favour of associations and bill-sticking or not he ain't gonna let a thing like that lay. Clay's a stickler for duty.'

Sally said: 'I was coming out of Mrs Murphy's when Brad came down the street — '

'Riding?'

'No, he was walking.'

'Strange for that young man to walk. He likes to prance around on that grey of his.'

'Oh, Dad, you've got something to say about everything,' said Sally with an exasperation which would have been comic were it not so sincere. 'Maybe he left his horse at the edge of town.'

'What — an' groundhitched him? There ain't no livery stables there!'

'Well, maybe he had been in town a while and was walking around.'

'Maybe he was. Maybe the sheriff'll find out where he went after he lcft you.'

The girl choked back an angry retort. Her kindly father could be maddening at times. But her reason told her that his orneriness was due to the fact that he was as savage as a man of his temperament could be over the ill-use of his friend. She must go easy.

'Brad said, 'Good afternoon,' and asked if he could talk with me for a moment.'

'He can do the gent all right, I'll say that for him.'

'He asked me if he could take me to the barbecue on Saturday.'

'An' what did you say?'

'I said 'Yes' — and why not?'

The old man snorted but did not answer her question. The three of them passed through the alley, which was now deserted, and on to the main drag. There was no sign of the sheriff, Sol, or the doctor.

Luke Sands hopped towards them. 'Howdy Miss Sally,' he said.

The girl greeted him. Her father said: 'Anything cropped up, Luke?'

The bean-pole shook his head vigorously, setting his unruly hair a-bobbing. 'Not a thing. The sheriff's still questioning folks.'

'He knows why Sol was hit. He ought to know where the trouble lies.'

'He don't like the way things are turnin' out. You printin' any more o' them bills, John?'

'Yes. They'll be ready tonight if you

16

want to give a hand in distributing them.'

This time Luke nodded his head slowly. 'I dunno. I'm all for the Association — you know that, John — but I got Lucy an' the kids to think about.'

'Suit yourself, Luke.' The old man's voice was kindly.

'I'll think about it.' Luke made for the saloon. Then he suddenly spun on his heels again. 'Hey, John, a saddle-tramp jest rode in. He says John Harding is in Tombstone. He killed a couple o' men in the International.'

'I know, I got the message.'

'All we want now is for John Harding to come ridin' into Trinity Valley.' *Yeah, that's all we want.* Shaking his head mournfully Luke continued on his way.

2

The evening edition of the *Trinity Valley Times* was on the streets. The general opinion was that it packed a wallop bigger than anything that old John had printed yet — and that was saying something! The old man stuck his neck out higher than a Christmas turkey's. Those who feared the biting truth of his men derided him; his friends feared for him.

His editorial this time was longer than usual. Its tenor was similar to many he had written of late. But this time he was more outspoken. Again he lashed out at the landowners who wanted to grab all and would not let the small ranchers live in peace: who used their power and money to juggle with the law, and their strength in men and arms to procure 'accidents' such as had happened to Sol Murphy. John did not mention any names with that — he was canny. But in the next column he derided those who were outspoken enemies of the newly-formed Cattlemens' Association. He mentioned *their* names and left the reader to draw his own conclusions.

In the next breath he crowed that the association was growing. Yes, despite intimidation, threats and law-suits, and the rest, it was still growing. It was brought about by something which, despite their riches, the landowners, being hogs and rattlesnakes, would never understand. Apropos of their 'might is right' doctrine, John Mowbree deplored the fact that fast-shooting men with notches on their guns were the heroes of the day. Had people already forgotten the old pioneers who fought and toiled and suffered to make their wild Western land a place in which to live? Why, the Indians, against whom they had fought were better men than some of these Western 'troubadours and laughing soldiers of fortune'. (Here he quoted from a blurb in an Eastern paper). Had George Washington, he asked been 'quick on the draw,' had Abraham Lincoln, or Thomas Payne, or any others of that great army of fighters for freedom and tolerance? That was a fine flourishing conclusion to a leader.

The main item of news was on page two. The John Harding shooting affray in the International Saloon in Tombstone. Since then, Mowbree had received another message hotfoot from Brodie. A kid named Sanderson, who had been making quite a name for himself as a pistoleer, had challenged Harding's right to call himself the 'fastest gun in the West'. He had drawn and Harding had beaten him easily. His elder brother, who had suddenly decided to try and get the famous gunman from behind, had shared a like fate.

Two men dead, and John Harding still unscathed. Boy, that was something! Maybe he'd come this way and they'd have a chance to get a look at him. Jack Carless, relief barman at the Proud Valley Saloon, who had seen Harding in action at Abilene, was in demand and had more to drink than was good even for a soaker like him.

Sheriff Hosell said that if Harding did come, and if there was any flag-waving and whooping-up, he'd fill the jail quicker than you could spit and with John Harding in the middle of 'em if need be. And Clay Hosell was famous for keeping his word.

Then there was old John Mowbree's editorial. It was said that in his youth John could bring tears to men's eyes with the eloquence of his persuasive pen. Times had changed, the flamboyant and sentimental verbiage of those days was outdated, was lost on many. But John had lost little of his old touch and many a man in the Proud Valley Saloon that night, in reading his editorial, felt a rekindling of old idealism or maybe an uneasy sense of something else, something left to slide, something left undone. Known supporters of the Cattlemens' Association were loud in the old man's praises but it was noticeable that no other names were mentioned — though the editorial was choc-a-bloc with them. Other folks, less voluble, were of the opinion that old John was riding for a fall.

In the print-shop the yellow lights were still burning, the press continued to rattle and rumble. The latter was worked by old John himself, for Sam Garner, protesting vehemently, had long since been sent home.

Sally stood at the typecase, her nimble fingers placing the little metal pieces into her setting-stick with almost unbelievable rapidity. Her goldy-brown hair was tied back into a severe bun at the back of her head with a piece of red ribbon. She wore a flowered apron tied tightly at the waist, enhancing the curves of her figure. Her face was set and beautiful beneath the light, her eyes shadowed. She looked very grave, very resolute.

There were no blinds on the windows of the shop and the girl could be clearly seen from outside. Maybe that was why cowboys went by at repeated intervals — until old John was wearied by their passing.

'What do they think this is — a zoo?' he said.

The third occupant of the print-shop spoke up then. 'I'll give some o' the monkeys the length of me tongue,' he said with unconscious aptness.

He was big and his raven-black hair was almost entirely hidden by swathes of white bandages. Sol Murphy had come a little early to collect his bills and was helping John to get them off the press.

He strode to the door and flung it open.

'Please don't start any trouble, Sol,' called John Mowbree.

The girl looked up too but said nothing. Her blue eyes shone in the light and there was a hint of devilment in them. Sol stood, arms akimbo, just outside the door. A man came along. He passed the windows before he came to the door. He craned his neck and peered. His gaze flitted across the bent head of John Mowbree and rested on the figure of the girl at the typerack. He was so interested in what he saw that he did not notice the big Irishman until he had almost barged into him. He was a little man. He darted around Sol like a terrier and sped down the street.

Sol bawled: 'Ain't yuh got nothin' else to do?' His voice died away as he heard laughter and saw two more men approaching. Just let them gawp that was all and Begob he'd show 'em! He clenched his huge fist and dodged back into the shelter of the doorway.

The heavy boot-heels sounded nearer. When they were almost on top of him he darted from cover. He ran into the two men and one of them grabbed him. He swung a fist, felt it connect. The man went sprawling from the broadwalk. Sol turned on the other one, but he stopped dead when a voice

24

said: 'Is it crazy you are, yuh big slob?'

Then his arms were pinioned but he took it all with surprising mildness. He did not even struggle or speak: it was his turn to gawp. The first man picked himself up out of the dust and climbed on to the boardwalk once more. He said: 'What's the idea? I ought to beat your face in, you big ape.'

'I'm sorry, boys,' said Sol weakly. 'I didn't know it was you. Folks've bin comin' by all night, staring in, lookin' at Miss Sally. I thought — '

'Stickin' your neck out again, uh?' said the first man. He rubbed his jaw ruefully. 'That knock on the head didn't have any effect on your punch. I guess you're fit enough to take a beatin' back o' the barn later.'

Sol tore himself away from the other's grasp. 'A beatin' is it. Who's gonna help yuh, yuh young coxcomb? I'll thrash you right here with one hand behind me back. I will!'

'You'll need both of 'em, me bucko,' said his opponent as he advanced.

The other man suddenly stepped in between them. 'Cut it out, you two,' he said. 'Now isn't the time to be fighting.' He turned sharply towards Sol. 'When we got in Ma told us where you'd gone an' about how you got bopped. We came along to see if you'd be wantin' any help.'

'Yeah, an' a ferocious attack on our persons is all the thanks we get,' grumbled the one behind him.

Instantly Sol was all contrition once more. 'I'm sorry, boys,' he said.

He flung his arms around the shoulders of both of them. He kicked the print-shop door open. 'Folks,' he carrolled: 'Me brothers have come to help me.'

'Welcome, boys,' said John Mowbree as the trio entered the shop.

Sally looked up too and her white teeth flashed as she grinned. Sol's brothers, the younger, Pat, and the elder, Manny, stood a little sheepishly on the threshold and doffed their hats. Pat, who was still brushing himself down after his tumble, was taller even than Sol but less lummoxy. He was wide shouldered and rangy and dark as an Indian. His smile was slower than Sally's but his teeth flashed as brilliantly in his handsome face.

Manny, who was seven years older than Sol and approaching middle-age, was sluggish of movement and running to fat. He was good-humoured and slower to anger than the other two. His plump red face was barred in half by a huge black moustache. He said: 'We bin out on the farm all day. We didn't hear nothin' o' the shindig till we got back an hour ago. As soon as we'd had some chow we came right along.'

Pat said: 'Has the sheriff got the one who hit yuh yet, Sol?'

Sol made a disgusted sound. 'Not him. He might've done it himself.'

'Now, Sol, you know you don't mean that,' said John Mowbree mildly.

Pat said 'We dropped in the Proud Valley for a quick one as we came along. In there we heard that Brad

Simmons was in town when you got bopped.'

There was an awkward silence. Then Sally said: 'Just about the time Sol got 'bopped', as you call it, Brad Simmons was talking to me outside your home.'

'That clears him I guess,' said Manny.

'He was just waiting for his boys to finish the job they came to do,' said Sol.

John Mowbree said: 'In all fairness to everybody concerned I must tell you that none of Brad Simmons' pards were in town today.'

Nobody said anything to that. Sol was busy stacking bills once more, Pat was glowering at Sally's bent head, and Manny stood seemingly irresolute in the middle of the floor.

John said briskly: 'Soon be ready now, boys.'

Pat went over to Sally and stood watching her as she fed the type into the setting stick. She was engrossed in her work, she did not seem to have noticed his approach. There was a maddening grace about her. He tapped his foot impatiently, then he spoke her name. She looked up and smiled.

'Just a minute, Pat,' she said. 'Let me finish this line.'

He shrugged and pouted like a child. But she did not see his annoyance for her head was bent once more over her work and, as he watched her, the sullen lines of his face softened again. Half unconsciously he stretched out his hand, but it stopped before it reached its objective and fell limply to his side. Emotion struggled across Pat's dark, mobile face but pride and temper overlay them all. The latter emotion was getting the upper hand when Sally put down her setting-stick and looked up.

'Did you want to say something, Pat?'

The man was showered by the blue, sparkling warmth of her eyes and he swallowed his bile, nevertheless his face was a little flushed when he said: 'Are you going to the barbeque, Sally?'

'Yes, I am.'

Some of Pat's native courtesy returned to him. He made a bow. 'You'll be wanting an escort then. May I have the honour?'

The girl's eyes clouded, she bit her lip. She looked down at the typecase, as if seeking something there, then she looked up at Pat once more.

'I'm sorry,' she said. 'I've promised to go with someone else.' He did not speak and she went on hurriedly.

'I'll save some dances for you. If you had asked me earlier — '

Pat interrupted her. 'Who's takin' you?'

'When I met Brad Simmons this afternoon he asked me.'

'You're goin' with that fancy-talkin' sidewinder — the man who — '

'Don't say any more, Pat. Don't say anything you'll be sorry for.'

As her voice lashed him Pat stopped dead in the middle of his tirade. When he went on his voice was soft, but he stood over the girl almost, as if he meant to strike her.

'All right, if that's what you want. But Mr Brad Simmons had better watch his step.' He spun on his heels and crossed the room in long strides. As he passed the others he said, 'If you want me I'll be in the Proud Valley.' Then the door banged behind him.

Manny said: 'I'll follow him. We don't want him on the rampage now.'

He disappeared in the wake of Pat. Sol looked at Sally. She returned his glance defiantly then carried on with her work.

John Mowbree said hurriedly, 'Wal, I think that's the lot.' He stopped the press, stacked up the papers with expert hands. 'Got your bag, Sol?'

'Yeah, I got it.' Sol handed him a canvas gunny sack.

John dropped the bills into it. 'Take care, I'll be out after you as soon as I've got this other page run off.'

'Ye don't hafta do that. You stay right here.' Sol took the sack in a huge hand and made for the door. As he advanced the drumming of hooves in the street became a frenzied clatter. Sol stopped dead at the violence of the sound. Then he said, 'Fool cowboys,' and carried on.

He had reached the door when the bunch of horsemen drew abreast with the print-shop. Glass crashed and tinkled as stones ripped through the windows. Old John threw up his hands to protect his eyes. With a cry Sally ran towards him. She staggered as a stone hit her shoulder. Then she plunged on.

Sol drew his gun and flung open the door. The last of the riders were disappearing in the gloom. Sol's lips were drawn back from his teeth as he levelled his gun. He fired and one of the riders threw up his arms and crashed from his mount. The others thundered on and disappeared. From the other end of the street men came running.

Sol went back into the print-shop. 'John — Sally — you all right?'

Father and daughter stood side by side. They both nodded wordlessly. Then the girl said, 'Who was it?'

'I dunno, but I got one of them.'

Boot-heels thudded on the board-walk. The door swung and Clay Hosell came in. He looked around him at the shattered windows, the debris on the floor. Outside the door a voice said: 'There's one of 'em lyin' in the middle of the street, sheriff.'

Without a word Hosell turned and went back through the door.

'I guess I'd better go see who I've shot,' said Sol and followed him.

Father and daughter were left alone and exchanged worried glances. The old man indicated the damage with a wave of his hand.

'All this can be fixed,' he said. 'But that shot can't. I wish Sol hadn't fired it. I hope the man, whoever he is, isn't hurt badly.

'I'm not blaming Sol, my dear.' The old man's voice was suddenly weary. As he took off his apron and donned his jacket he said: 'Seems like no man can fight clean nowadays.'

The door opened again and Sam Garner came in. His eyes lit up with relief as he saw them both standing there unscathed.

John said: 'Stay with Sally while I go down the street.'

'Yes, sir.'

'Oh no, you don't,' said the girl. 'I'm going with you.' She flung her plaid coat around her shoulders and stepped towards the door. It opened and Pat Murphy burst in. 'Sally — are you all right?' He caught hold of her shoulders.

For a moment they were both motionless, he looming over her, personification of protection, she looking up at him, eyes wide, lips slightly parted. Then the spell was broken and she shrugged away from him saying, 'Yes, I'm all right. Go back to your drinking, Pat.'

It was a cruel thrust, and the young Irishman did not notice the sudden, shakiness of the husky voice. He only heard the words. His face flushed deeply. He turned away from her abruptly and the swinging door hit his temple with a sharp crack. He staggered back from it with a cry of pain. Her eyes wide, Sally caught his arm.

'Pat — I'm sorry. I didn't mean to be nasty. It was just that you kind of startled me.'

He rubbed his forehead and looked down at her. Then his sullen face slowly crinkled and he began to laugh. Sally held his arm and his body shook with laughter. She began to laugh with him, her high pointed breasts straining the cloth of her shirtwaist as she threw her head back.

John Mowbree said: 'When you two jackasses have quit blocking the door maybe I can get out.'

They moved aside automatically and he passed them with young Sam in his wake. They went down the street and left the man and the girl behind them, laughing in the lit-up shambles of the print-shop.

They stopped laughing abruptly, and their faces were very close together. Then Pat bent his head, and they kissed for quite a long time.

'Are you still goin' to the barbeque with Brad Simmons?' he asked.

'We shouldn't be here,' said the girl breathlessly. 'Things are happening. We — '

'I asked you a question.'

'A promise is a promise,' she said.

Pat began to kiss her again.

3

John Mowbree and young Sam were ahead of the stream of people coming in increasing volume from the vicinity of the Proud Valley and kindred spots. When they got to the man in the roadway there were only Sol, Manny, the sheriff, and three other men collected around him.

'He's dead all right,' said the sheriff. 'The slug hit him plumb in the middle o' the back. Who fired the shot?'

'I did,' said Sol. 'You saw what they did to the print-shop.'

'Who is it?' said John Mowbree.

'Cal Prentiss, a Silver Star man.' The sheriff flung the information over his shoulder. He faced the big Irishman. He said: 'I'll have to hold yuh, Sol.'

'What for? I'm sorry I killed the man — but he asked for it.'

'Sorry, Sol.' The sheriff began to move forward.

Sol was uncertain. He had respect for the law and, in this case, the man who represented it. He backed a little, his hand moving uncertainly. The crowd, which had gotten thicker, began to back out. The centre circle became suddenly wider.

'Sol,' said John Mowbree warningly.

Sol ignored him but looked at his brother. 'Everything's gonna be all right,' said Manny stolidly and did not move.

The sheriff moved nearer. 'Don't start any trouble, Sol.'

Sol looked around him again. Maybe he was seeking Pat, less stolid than Manny, less law-abiding. But Pat was nowhere to be seen. The sheriff moved suddenly closer, crowding Sol so that he could not reach for his gun. From the crowd behind the Irishman a little man stepped and jabbed a gun in Sol's back.

The big man became rigid. 'Dirty

sons of bitches,' he said.

'Up with 'em, Sol,' said the little man, and the gun jabbed again.

Sol slowly raised his hands, the little man took his gun.

'Hey,' said Manny, and began to move.

The sheriff's draw was very fast. He covered the elder brother. 'Don't mess things up, Manny,' he said. 'This has got to be done.'

'Mind how you handle Sol, sheriff,' said Manny sombrely.

Hosell ignored the underlying threat. He nodded and his voice was level as he said, 'You know me.' Then he raised it. 'Open up there! The show's over!'

Soapy Sanders, the undertaker, and his assistant, Jake, were carting the body away. The sheriff and the little man, who was his deputy, Lew Connors, shepherded their prisoner in the wake of the man he had killed.

As they passed the print-shop Sally and Pat came out. Both of them took in the situation with a glance. Pat went for his gun.

The cavalcade which streamed behind the party scattered right and left. Lew Connors started forward like a terrier. The undertaker and his man dropped the body in the dust once more and dived for cover. Then tragedy was averted as Sally hung on Pat's arm and, her face white and strained in the streaming light, spoke to him urgently.

Sheriff Hosell caught his deputy's arm. The killing trance dropped from Pat like a cloak. He let his hands fall and the girl beside him went limp. He looked at her as if he had never seen her before.

Somebody laughed then, pointing at the body in the road as Soapy Sanders and Jake slunk from hiding to take it up once more. In a moment the street rocked with laughter and the crowd jostled behind the undertakers and their burden, the law and their prisoner, as they passed on down the street.

A queer little smile played around

Pat's lips as he looked down at the girl once more. 'They won't keep my brother,' he said. Then he left her.

She let him go, but there was fear in her eyes as she watched him disappear in the gloom. Terrors were clustering around her, increasing all the time. She was glad when her father joined her, and, Sam, and Manny, who carried Sol's bulging gunny sack.

'I'll see to this little chore, John,' he said. As the old man thanked him he was already walking away in the wake of the crowd, in the opposite direction to the one his youngest brother had taken.

Sally lingered. She looked along the street. There was no movement up there now. Lights from scattered cabins glowed dimly. Beyond them was the range, but there was no indication of the place where it met the sky. The stars were very high and gave little light. Out there were no answers to her questions, and as her father called her name Sally turned and followed him and Sam into the glass-bestrewed shop.

'Get along home, Sam,' said old John. 'There's nothing you can do here, Sally and I have nearly finished. Go on, I say! Your maw will be worried about you.'

'Oh, all right,' said the youth, and slouched through the door.

Sally said: 'Mebbe I ought to follow him and see that he goes straight home.'

'He'll be all right. He'll go straight home. He thinks more of his old maw than he lets on to.'

The old man went on reflectively: 'Seems to me that the younger generation think its being soft to appear to love and honour their parents. I don't know what the world's coming to Sally.'

The girl could not suppress the laugh which bubbled up huskily from the depths of her throat. She said breathlessly: 'I guess I'll be saying just the same things when I'm your age.'

'Guess you will, girl. I always say — ' John broke off as hoof-beats clattered in the street. They stopped outside. The old man crossed to the press, reached behind it and produced a shotgun. He levelled it at the door as it opened.

The man who entered stopped dead in astonishment. 'What's been goin' on here?'

'Oh, it's you, Henny.' John lowered his gun.

Henny had a round face and no eyebrows. He was a picture of amazement as he stood and looked around him. 'A bunch of hooligans've been throwing rocks,' said John. He was suddenly peevish, 'What can I do for you, Henny?'

'I'm sorry about this, Mr Mowbree!' said the cowboy. 'Gosh, that must've been what all the ruckus was about down the street.'

'A man got shot.'

'Who?'

'One o' your pards, Cal Prentiss.'

'Who done it?'

'They'll tell you all about it down at the Proud Valley I guess.'

'Yeah,' said Henny half to himself. Then his voice burst out again. 'I've bin to Tombstone, Mr Mowbree, on a job for the boss. As I was coming away Big Brodie gave me an envelope for you.'

He began to fumble inside his tattered dust-stained vest. Finally he produced a crumpled envelope and held it out.

John took it, saying: 'Your boss wouldn't like you bringing messages to me, Henny.'

'Aw, Mr Mowbree, the boss ain't thet bad. Anyway, I don't mind doin' a favour for a couple o' gents.'

'That's mighty nice of you, Henny.'

'Shucks, it ain't nuthin'.' Henny stood uncertainly as the old man and the girl stood regarding him without speaking. He gave the latter a belated salute. Then he began to turn, mumbling, 'Pore Cal, I guess I'd better go an' hear all about it. Cal was wild, but that wasn't any call for anybody to go an' shoot him.'

'Goodnight, Henny,' said John.

After he had gone, the old man said: 'Brodie's a fool to send any Tom, Dick and Harry here with messages. Good job it was only a simpleton like Henny. Any other of the Silver Star men would have ridden right to Jasper Hart — or Brad Simmons — with that envelope.'

'You hadn't used to be so suspicious-minded, Dad. Not until you got in so deep with this Cattlemens' Association. And you not even a cattleman.'

'No, I never had, had I?' said John, half to himself. 'And I'm not a cattleman either.' Then his voice rose. 'But all my life I've been trying to do what's right. I've always stood for justice and fair dealing, and I would be a poor newspaperman if I didn't. I'm against Jasper Hart and the rest of them — and all their kind.'

There was a dewy tenderness in the girl's eyes as she watched him; pride, and a queer uneasiness too. She knew he was right. The old gentle warrior had always been right — and she could only hope that the cantankerousness and suspicions of his old age would not force him into hasty action. She feared for him. He was her father; he was so dear, so old. Too old, in more ways than one, for the cynical times he so repeatedly deplored.

He stood in the middle of the floor and his voice had stopped, but his head was still uplifted and there was that old light in his eyes. She said gently: 'Open the envelope, Dad, and see what Brodie has to say.'

He came to himself, his eyes blinked into hers. 'Yes, he said, and turned the envelope over and over.

His hands were trembling as he inserted his thumb in the flap. The envelope tore raggedly and the small folded piece of paper fell to the floor. The old man held the empty envelope. The girl stepped forward and picked up the paper. She unfolded it and looked at the message.

Her head was downcast. The old man watched her anxiously. 'Read it out,' he said.

'Brodie says: *John Harding has left Tombstone and is moving in your direction.*'

The girl's voice died away. Father and daughter looked at each other. In both pairs of blue eyes there was anguish. And something more, which would have been undefinable to anyone else: its meaning known only to themselves.

4

Pat Murphy sat on a boulder on the side of the trail just behind town. Behind him he could hear the small creek, which was the main source of water in the valley, gurgling merrily. But his thoughts were not merry; they were black, and he was wrestling against their attempt to overpower him.

His gun was on his lap. He had been checking it, with a devilish purpose in his mind, when reason took a hand. Now, slowly, it had been forgotten, and he was looking off into the blackness, seeing a piquant face with blue eyes and goldy-brown smoke of hair, almost feeling those soft hands on him, that soft body pressed to his, those warm lips . . .

He gave a muttered half humorous curse and, rising, holstered his gun. He took a couple of steps forward then he stopped, listening. The breeze soughed, the creek gurgled, and, above it all, a steady drumming sound came. Fast at first, then slowing down as it came nearer.

Pat moved back to the fringe of the cottonwoods along the creek and concealed himself there. His gun was out again and he listened and peered and waited.

The rider loomed up out of the darkness, the sparse light of the stars etched his tall figure for a moment, and that of his big rawboned horse, so that they looked enormous. Then the man turned his mount. He was making straight for Pat and the Irishman's finger was taut on the trigger of his gun when, at a word from the rider, the horse stopped.

The man dismounted and stretched himself. He was not so tall as Pat, and probably leaner, but there was the same ranginess about him. He looked towards the cottonwoods, his head moving, taking his fill of the sight of them. For a second it seemed he was looking straight at the place where Pat was concealed. The Irishman was on the point of stepping out when the man turned away. He spoke softly to the horse then seated himself on the rock Pat had just vacated.

The horse passed his master and wandered through the trees to the edge of the creek, close to Pat, and the young man was thankful he had not brought his own mount with him. The stranger rolled himself a quirly, sat smoking on the rock and looking down at the lights of the town.

The horse, having drank his fill, turned away from the creek and ran right upon the motionless Pat. It snorted and backed away in terror. The stranger whirled around. Pat said: 'Hold it, pardner, I've got you covered. Up with the mitts! Up with them I say!'

The man raised his hands to the level of his ten-gallon hat. Pat stepped out of cover and advanced towards him. 'I don't mean you no harm, pardner, but

I don't like fast movements so don't make any more of 'em.'

'You hold all the aces, pardner,' said the other. His voice was deep, harsh, mocking. There was a hint of latent savagery in it and Pat knew he must go wary.

'Who are yuh?'

'Jest a saddle-tramp passing through. Who are you? — what were yuh doin' skulking back there?'

Pat grinned. His black mood was gone. He was cocky; he felt no malice against this tall stranger, whoever he was.

He said: 'I came up here for a smoke. I heard yuh comin an' dodged out of sight. Sorry I jumped out on yuh but, like I said, I don't like fast movements.' He went closer to the man, seeing the lean outlines of his face, the quirk of his lips, half mocking, half friendly. The man said: 'Can I drop my hands? I promise not to make any fast movements — an' I don't bite.'

Pat chuckled deep in his throat. 'All

right. Drop 'em slowly to the middle of your belt.'

'Mind if I sit down? I'm kinda saddle-sore.'

Pat nodded. 'Go ahead.' He was still taut, watchful: so much could happen in an encounter like this. The stranger did not look vicious but he was tough, rangy, and Pat remembered that whirling movement, like the turnabout spring of a cougar.

'Easy, stranger,' he said softly. 'Easy.'

The man relaxed with a little sigh. His hands close together, covering the silver buckle of his belt. Pat wondered whether he ought to make him drop his gun-belt, draw his fangs entirely, and make him powerless. The cockiness in him, the pride, as well as a latent sense of fairplay made him shrink from taking that step. He had the drop on the man, what more did he want?

As if echoing his thoughts the stranger said: 'Your move, pardner.'

Pat grinned and holstered his gun. 'Mebbe you're the ghost of Bill Hickok himself,' he said. 'But I'll take a chance,' then, seeing the stranger's answering grin, he went on: 'Sorry I jumped yuh. Don't do to take no chances nowadays.' He jerked a little as the other man's hand moved. But the stranger was only reaching up to his upper vest pocket. He brought out a small sack of 'makings' and tossed it. Pat caught it deftly.

He took out a paper and spilled baccy on to it. His eyes were on the man all the time and the look was returned. Both were half-smiling, measuring each other up feature by feature, seeking each other in the darkness.

Pat held the sack in one hand, rolled the quirly with finger and thumb of the other. He stuck it between his lips. He tightened the string at the mouth of the sack and tossed it back. The man caught it.

Pat got matches from his vest-pocket, took one and lit up. He watched the stranger make a smoke for himself then, when he was ready, tossed him the small book of matches.

The stranger lit up; Pat received the matches back and sidled off a little to lean against a tree. He said: 'Goin' into Trinity Valley?'

'This *is* Trinity Valley, ain't it?'

'The town I mean.'

'Ain't thought about it. I might do. I might not. Might just pass by on the ridge. Anythin' worth seein' in the town?'

'No more than in any other little Western burg I guess. Usual saloons, gambling houses, and what not. Stores, a bank, newspaper office an' print-shop — ain't every town that's got a newspaper — '

'It ain't. What do you find for news in a one-horse town like that?'

'It ain't all that little,' said Pat a little peevishly. 'There's big ranches all around; cowboys whoopin' it up; we have our shootings.' He was on the point of telling the stranger that they had had one that very night, but he checked himself. He was talking too much. The gink might be a lawman or, on the other hand, a hold-up man. He had a mighty persuasive tongue, so Pat concluded abruptly: 'You lookin' for a job, mister?'

'Not particularly. Jest roamin'. Could use one soon I guess. Anythin' good goin' around here?'

'There's three big ranches the other side town. The Silver Star, the Lame W, and the Circle 6. There's lots o' smaller spreads an' farms too that might be able to use an extra hand this time of the year, somebody who don't mind hard work.'

Pat was thinking that his family could use one at their own little farm, but still he was not sure of this tall ranny. Both men remained silent for a time. The stranger spoke suddenly in that slow, harsh, but persuasive drawl of his. 'I'll jest mosey along I guess. Maybe I'll stay, maybe I won't.' He rose slowly.

Pat watched him, a little irritated by his lackadaisical demeanour. Well, to hell with him if he didn't want to be helped. The man threw away the stub of his cigarette and stretched himself. His gestures were almost arrogant.

'Will you excuse me a minute, pardner?' he asked, adding, 'I'll go fill my water-canteen an' get my hoss. Guess you've scared the lights out of him! He ain't used to strange men.' There was that mocking note in his voice again.

It riled Pat. He said, 'Don't let me stop you doin' nothin', stranger. I was goin' back to town anyway.'

'Mebbe I'll follow you,' said the man. 'Maybe I'll see you later. I guess a town that runs a newspaper is worth seein'. What's the newspaper called, pardner?'

'*The Trinity Valley Times.*'

'Who prints it?'

So persuasive was that voice that Pat found himself answering again almost unconsciously. 'An old man and his daughter. John Mowbree an' Sally.'

'A purty gel?'

'Yeah, mighty purty. An' a friend o' mine, mister.'

'No offence, pardner.' The tall man moved towards the trees.

'I'll get on. Maybe I'll see you again.'

'Maybe. *Adios, amigo.*'

'*Adios.*'

As Pat descended the slope to the town there was a prickly feeling down his spine. Varied emotions chased themselves across his mind but pride was uppermost. He still did not trust that stranger, was piqued and irritated by him; but not until he was moving into the main drag did he look back, and then he could see nothing but darkness. The cottonwoods were hidden in the gloom, and the stranger and his horse with them. Pat was left wondering whether he would meet that tall rather mysterious man again and learn something about him.

There were lots of folks in the aura of light which came from the Proud Valley Saloon and other establishments of the same kind in the centre of the town. Pat moved in amongst them. On the steps of the saloon a big cowhand was shooting off his mouth. Pat recognized him as a Silver Star ranny named Carmody. He saw more Silver Star men gathered around, as well as employees of the other big ranches, the Lame W and Circle 6. Pat figured some of these men must have been in the wild party who smashed the windows of the print-shop. They had probably filtered into town in twos and threes. It was evident that they had heard of the killing of the Silver Star ranny, Cal Prentiss. Such was the subject of Carmody's harangue. But he was not having it all his own way: he was being barracked by townsmen. There was an atmosphere of good humoured truculence which in some quarters was on the verge of breaking into something more serious.

'Shot in the back!' bawled Carmody. Pat had heard him use the same phrase three times and he had probably used it before that. He had powerful lungs but he was not a good orator, and a wizened little townsman on the edge of the crowd was pecking at him like a hen at a worm.

'Prentiss attacked private property, didn't he? An' he was shot at in doin' so. It's the right of every house-holder or shopkeeper to protect his holdings in any way he thinks fit — that's what the law says about it!'

'The print-shop don't belong to Sol Murphy!'

'No, but he was protecting it. There was a female there — he was protecting her too. It's any man's right to protect womenfolk. If we're gonna allow drunken cowboys to ride around an' throw rocks at our women-folk we'll soon be a damsight worse than Tombstone.'

'Yep, that's right,' yelled somebody else. 'It was jest Prentiss's bad luck that he was the one to get shot. I didn't notice that any of his pards turned back to pick him up. They were too damn' scared for their own hides.'

'Who was scared?' yelled somebody in the centre of the crowd.

The voice rang above the general babble and silence followed suddenly as everybody turned to find its source. But in the rapidly growing crowd this was not easy particularly as the shouter was probably surrounded by his pals.

Carmody created another diversion by bawling: 'Prentiss was just a wild cowboy — he never done anybody any harm. His gun was still in his holster, fully loaded and untouched. He was murdered by a back-shooting skunk. I'll say it again: Sol Murphy is a filthy back-shootin' skunk an' ought to be hung higher'n a kite. Are we gonna stand for one of our pards bein' shot in the back? That sheriff's laughin' at us. As soon as we're out o' town he'll let his prisoner free.'

There were shouts from all sides then. This was lynch talk! Heads swayed back and forth. Pat Murphy moved through the crowd towards Carmody. He was not going to stand by and hear his brother called a back-shooting skunk. His blood was up again, and the pride of the Murphys kept him going. He'd ram those words down Carmody's throat if it was the last thing he did.

Men began to notice his approach, to move aside to let him through.

'Watch yourself, Pat,' said somebody.

'Here's one of the Murphys who ain't in jail,' yelled another.

Carmody, with his red choleric face and sandy hair, glowered down at the approaching figure. Men moved away a little from the edge of the boardwalk and the big ranny was left standing alone.

'No shooting for Pete's sake,' said somebody as Carmody's hand hovered over the butt of his gun.

The big man realized the speaker's wisdom. There were too many people about, packed too close together. And Carmody himself was a sitting duck, silhouetted there in the light.

Pat reached the edge of the board-walk and Carmody leaned forward and swung at him with a ham-like fist. Pat stepped back and the blow swung past him. Carmody teetered on the edge of the planks. Pat moved in and drove a straight right to the big man's middle.

The crowd roared as Carmody doubled, his knees sagging. He tumbled forward into the street at Pat's feet. There was laughter and cheers.

But Carmody was tough. And the jeers whipped him into a frenzy. He rose, half-crouching, and charged forward. His hat rolled in the dust. His bullet head, like a battering ram, caught Pat in the chest. The crowd broke and the young Irishman flew backwards in their midst with Carmody after him like a charging bull.

The arena shifted. In a narrow cleft among shifting feet Pat and Carmody rolled ignominiously in the dust. Their legs kicked, their fists flailed. The crowd, all rancour swallowed up in watching this battle of giants.

Manny Murphy pushed his way to the front of the crowd. His gunny-sack was empty, his job was done. His solidity left him as he yelled at his brother to beat the big ranny to pulp. Pat was doing his best but at the moment, with the wind knocked out of him by Carmody's charge, he was bottom-dog.

Carmody was astride him, chopping away with both hands but so much was the Irishman squirming that many of his blows missed altogether and two or three times he hit the hard ground. Pat used his knees, jolting the big man forward over his head. In falling Carmody almost smothered him. Pat squirmed from under and rose swiftly to his feet.

He stood swaying and blowing. Carmody rose and flung himself forward once more, his fists up in a pugilistic stance. His left shot out and Pat blocked it, back-peddling a little and still blowing. Carmody followed him like a bulldog, throwing blows from all angles. No science but plenty of guts and power. Pat blocked them repeatedly, dodged, feinted, threw two sharp stinging blows at Carmody's face and dodged out of harm's way.

Carmody shook his head like an enraged terrier and continued to advance. He smashed a terrific blow through Pat's guard. The Irishman staggered, blood splashing from his face. Carmody went after him ferociously, his little eyes sparkling in the light. However, Pat was a seasoned brawler, and he fought automatically. He dodged the big man's rush and, crouching, blood still dropping from him flung a couple of round-arm blows to Carmody's middle. Carmody was brought up short, his grunts loud in the stillness. Then Pat was facing him, slinging punishing blows. A left beneath the heart, a right in the mouth, a left to the side of the head then, as Carmody teetered, a beautiful right to the point. Carmody's head went back, his heels left the floor. He crashed flat on his back. His big body, suddenly flabby, twitched once then became still.

5

Another man started from the crowd and launched himself at Pat from the side. The Irishman spun on his heels and swung a long aim. His fist exploded in the man's face. The man's boot-heels tore grooves in the hard dusty mud. He was caught by his pardners who surged forward, three of them with him teetering in their midst.

Manny Murphy ranged himself alongside his brother. The nearest cowboy had a damp empty gunny sack slapped in his face with stinging violence. Another one received a kick in the shins that knocked his left from under him and sent him howling to the ground. Manny had his own unorthodox methods, rough but very effective. The other member of the party hesitated as if beginning to change his mind. Pat, taking heart from Manny's performance, suddenly pounced on him, grabbed him by the throat, swung him around and planted a mighty kick to the seat of his pants. The man was precipitated into the midst of the yelling, laughing crowd. That crowds' temper was changing once more.

Manny had his arm around Pat's shoulders and they were turning when Carmody rose slowly to his feet. The big ranny looked around him, saw the man he sought and went for his gun. Pat pushed his brother out of the way, threw himself to the other side, his own hand moving downwards. But Carmody had the advantage of surprise. His gun boomed. The slug went over Pat's head and whistled over the heads of the crowd.

Pat was down on one knee. He winced as a slug nicked his arm. Then he fired coolly. The gun spun from the other man's hand. Carmody cried out and fell back, clutching his shoulder.

Pat menaced the crowd, his lips stretched in a faint snarl. Manny, his gun out now, stood beside him. Pards of Carmody crowded forward, shifting ominously.

'Watch it,' said Pat. 'Or by God I'll start blastin'.'

Another young man stepped suddenly into the clearest space. The light shone on his bare head, his flowing blond hair.

'Keep out o' this, Simmons,' snarled Pat.

'I ain't aimin' to argue with a levelled gun,' said the other.

He was handsome, too handsome maybe for a hard-working cowhand. Handsome, arrogant, and well-built, too. He turned his head and said, 'Catch hold of Carmody some of yuh. Then get movin'. Any Silver Star man left in town in half-an-hour's time 'ull get his walking papers. The boss's gonna be hoppin' mad when he hears about this shindig. Who started it?'

'That Murphy gink slugged Carmody.'

'That's a lie,' said Pat. Voices in the crowd backed him up.

In retaliation a Silver Star man shouted: 'Sol Murphy killed Cal Prentiss, Brad. Shot him in the back.'

'I heard about that,' said Brad Simmons. 'These smallholders are taking too much on themselves. This one'll hang!'

A roar greeted this. 'I vote we hang him right now,' shouted a man.

'Every damn Silver Star man'll get outa town right now,' bawled Brad Simmons. 'Or I'll want to know the reason why. What the rest o' you do is no concern o' mine.'

From behind him a voice said: 'I ought to shoot you down now like a dog, you fancy-lookin' buzzard. You like other people to do your dirty work, don't you? Your men smashed up the print-shop but you waited till the coast was clear before you showed yourself, didn't you?'

Simmons turned to face Pat Murphy, who still stood with levelled gun. The blond-haired man showed no trace of fear, there was almost contempt in his arrogance. He said: 'I've been on a trip. I ain't been in town since early this afternoon. I didn't know what had happened until I jest rode in. Because one of my men was among a bunch of drunken cowboys doesn't mean that I, or any other Silver Star men, had anything to do with the ruckus. Whatever Cal did, he didn't deserve to be murdered for it.'

Pat's fury suddenly dropped from him. 'That was a beautiful grandstand play,' he said. 'Very brave and indignant and noble. You know I won't shoot you down.' He holstered his gun swiftly and stepped forward, fists out once more.

Manny grabbed him, pinioned his arms, dragging him back. 'You've done enough wildcattin' for one night.'

Pat struggled. Other townsmen joined with Manny in holding him. Tall, limping Luke Sands said: 'Get your men outa town pronto, Simmons, before the 'ull place blows up.'

'Let him go,' said Pat Murphy. 'I'm

givin' him fair warnin' — next time he comes here he'd better come a-gunnin'.'

There was a sudden silence, broken only by the scrape of feet as they carried away the unconscious form of Carmody. Brad Simmons followed them. He turned and looked at Pat. 'You're drunk,' he said.

'You're yellow,' said the Irishman.

Simmons shrugged contemptuously and passed on.

A murmur came from the crowd. The man had been challenged and called yellow. Did he mean to take up that challenge? He gave no sign. He and his men passed into the gloom. A few moments later their horses took them out of town.

Now that the Silver Star faction, always the biggest of all, had gone, the rest of the cowhands, from the Lame W and the Circle 6, went back to their drinking. There was no more lynch-talk; not openly at least. The big ranch employees were now outnumbered by townsmen and smallholders, so they wisely held their peace.

* ★ ★ ★

The inquest on Cal Prentiss was to be held the following morning at eleven o'clock in the courtroom, which was by turns assembly-hall, dance-hall, social centre and closed-in market; and which stood on the edge of town. Judge Lynus presiding, the hall was full, and a larger crowd jostled outside. All the people from the ranches who could manage to get into town had done so. It was surprising how many there were, and the townsfolk and smallholders looked at them askance.

Inside the hall Brad Simmons, foreman of the Silver Star, sat with his boss, Jasper Hart, a cadaverous man who looked like a sky-pilot but who, besides knowing all there was to know about ranching, was a hard-headed business man and, some folks said, an utterly unscrupulous one. It was he, with his power and riches and acre upon acre of lush lands, who begrudged the smallholder any corner in which to raise a little stock, or till the earth for planting.

In other parts of the assembly sat fat Bill Runshon, owner of the Lame W, and huge grizzled old Curly Billock of the Circle 6.

The foremost members of the opposing side, the prime movers in the smallholders' rather grandiously titled Cattlemens' Association, were there in force too. This was no ordinary inquest on a cowboy killed in a brawl. There was a lot more behind it.

John Mowbree was there; and his daughter Sally; and Sam Garner, and lanky, yellow-haired Luke Sands; and Jenky, the garrulous old-timer from the livery-stables; and Pat and Manny Murphy.

Sol Murphy sat on the rostrum, and close to him sat Clay Hosell and his cocky little deputy, Lew Connors. On the other end of the rostrum sat plump

Doc Billings, as neutral as any man could be, and aiming to stay that way. It was his job to give the medical evidence, and no more, and that was what he meant to do. Anyway, this was not a court of law — the prisoner, Sol Murphy, was only there in the capacity of a witness.

Still, you never could tell with old Judge Lynus. He was quite capable of giving a verdict on the case right off to save time. Doctor Billings was a little uneasy. He knew the old judge was as unbiased as he himself was, but he wondered what effect the verdict, whatever it was (and he had his own opinion as to what it should be), would have on the rival factions here.

Sometimes, like the sheriff, he wished the Cattlemens' Association had never been formed and that John Mowbree's *Times* was not such an outspoken broadsheet. Things were pretty peaceful in Trinity Valley until all that started. Then he reflected that he was being unfair. Yes, things had been peaceful for him and his contemporaries in town, but they had not been the same with the smallholders. Strange things had happened.

The smallholders, like beasts in separate lairs, were suspicious of each other as well as of the big landowners. That is, until John Mowbree and one or two more straight-thinking people took them in hand and showed them the error of their ways, and got them together and formed the Cattlemens' Association, in which they were banded together en bloc against the big fellers.

Billings liked John Mowbree. A slothful man himself, he admired the other's forthrightness and fighting spirit, although he thought the printer went a little too far at times, and for all his gentle manner, was occasionally somewhat intolerant, and guilty of jumping to conclusions. He was sure that John, a single-minded idealist, was not aware of these traits in his own character. Idealists seldom are.

That girl of his! She was a thoroughbred too and very like her father. She owned no man master, not even him. The doctor hoped John's idealistic endeavours would not land him and the girl into serious trouble. There was badness in the air. A badness not of the body but of the mind. Doc Billings wiggled his fingers across his ample stomach and sighed deeply.

There was little chatter in the courtroom. Many people besides the doctor were treating their brains to a thinking-spell while they waited for the old judge to appear at the table in the centre of the rostrum. There was speculation as to which way the judge would jump — you never could tell with that old goat. In a Western society given up, as John Mowbree was wont to put it, to the hero-worship of gunmen, it was natural maybe that many minds should turn to thoughts concerning such things.

People were wondering whether Brad Simmons, tagging into town on the tail of his boss, would take up the gauntlet Pat Murphy had flung at him. And, if so, what the outcome would be. Pat was a fast-shooting young hellion, more of the black sheep of the Murphys than Sol; but Brad Simmons, for all his fancy ways, was no slouch. Had he the guts to make his play? That was the question. Since last night opinions were divided on that score.

That the place was alive with lawmen and 'big bugs' made things more interesting. Though that fact might dissuade both the boys from doing anything rash right now ... Further speculation was cut short by the sudden appearance of Judge Lynus.

He had a habit of making sudden entrances like this. He came through a back door, and in a moment was before the table, looming over the assembly like some huge stringy bird of prey, that mocking gleam in his eyes beneath the bushy overhanging eyebrows.

With time-honoured ceremony the assembled company rose to its feet. The judge regarded them for a moment. Then he picked up his little wooden hammer, and struck the table a resounding bang.

'Pray be seated, ladies and gentlemen,' he said.

Everybody sat down and after another pause the judge declared the inquest on Cal Prentiss duly opened. After that things moved fast, and pretty soon it became evident that the old man, after his custom, was holding a trial as well as an inquest. And in his own inimitable way, too, silencing any protest with a bang of his hammer and a glare of his fiery eyes and, if that did not do the trick, his roar, 'Who's runnin' this?' As *he* indubitably was, that question never failed to silence his critics.

The sheriff put the case forward in his usual unbiased manner. Then John Mowbree and Sally gave evidence. One or two more folks who had been on the scene just after the shooting, who had followed the bunch of horsemen, heard the crash of glass, and the shot, were called forward. The judge heard them all with little comment, then asked Sol Murphy to speak his piece. The Irishman did so — with admirable control.

After he sat down there was a buzz of talk and the judge banged with his hammer again for silence. When that was regained he bent his head and ruminated for a while. That was another trick of his and usually a prelude to one of his curt electrifying announcements.

Eventually it came. In the clipped, harsh, yet ringing tones which he kept for such occasions Judge Lynus said:

'I find that Cal Prentiss was killed when caught in the act of misusing other folks' property. It's a thing that could happen to any wild and drunken cowboy, regrettable, unforeseen, but entirely just. I have examined a few of the rocks which crashed through the window of the print-shop.' He indicated them on the table before him. 'Any of them striking in the right place could have killed a man — or a woman. Miss Mowbree was indeed hit on the shoulder by one of them, and any man there was honour bound to protect her from further assault. Sol Murphy's action was hasty, I am of the opinion that he did not shoot to kill. I find him not guilty of murder, manslaughter or any criminal intent.'

There was clapping and cheers from some parts of the room, and cries of dissent from others. The judge glared and banged his table. 'Silence!' he thundered.

The babble died but there was still a murmuring undercurrent.

The judge said: 'I have a sneaking suspicion that the ride down main street last night and the smashing of the print-shop windows, was not just a cowboy prank, but a well-planned operation. Whatever people staged it have the blood of Cal Prentiss on their conscience, and I hope it will deter them from cooking up further plans of this sort.'

Something like a gasp went up from the assembly. The judge had not disappointed those who had come prepared for fireworks. It was characteristic of the fiery old man, who loved to see people hop, that he had the guts to put into words the thoughts that were in the minds of so many.

Judge Lynus banged his table once more. 'The circus is over,' he said. 'And I want no demonstrations.'

He turned and went through the back door. Outside his carriage was waiting, with Mose, his negro driver. A few seconds later the assembly heard it clattering away. People were stirring by then. Covert glances were thrown at Jasper Hart. He was the biggest landowner and Cal Prentiss had been his man. Had the attack on the print-shop been his plan too?

They failed to see the answer to the question in Hart's cadaverous features. Or even any inkling of what he thought of the judge's verdict. Townsfolk and smallholders, who were there in force, crowded around Sol Murphy to congratulate him. Clay Hosell and Deputy Lew Connors moved to the edge of the rostrum, obviously ready to meet trouble halfway if need be. Under the watchful eyes of their bosses, the dissenting cowhands filed sullenly out. If there was any symbol at all in this case, and many folks read one into it, it was an ignominious defeat for the landowners.

Jasper Hart, followed by Brad Simmons, got into his buckboard. The latter took the reins. The equipage rattled away, neither man giving a backward glance. Folk who had expected a gunfight were either relieved or disappointed. The Murphy brothers, coming out of the courtroom as the dust raised by Hart drifted away, made no comment.

6

Cal Prentiss was buried and forgotten. The print-shop windows were boarded up. The Cattlemens' Association held meetings. Their bills, dirtied and torn by weather, flapped in the breeze. Another edition of the *Trinity Valley Times*, which came out at spasmodic intervals, was expected. Things were pretty quiet, week-days. No more wild cowboys, no more shooting. But there was an atmosphere of waiting. Then came another weekend. The weekend of the barbecue.

This was held annually on the meadow on the north side of town. It was open house, and the admission was only ten cents. Many people who had looked upon the affair as one of jolly-making and good fellowship were not so keen on it this time. The cowhands from the big ranches might use it as an excuse to get a little of their own back. All the womenfolk would be there — but many of those young hellions had no respect for the fair sex.

Still, some of the landowners themselves might turn up: of yore they had been the guests of honour. That was before the bulk of the homesteaders came, before many of the townsfolk branched out into land outside town, and the landowners tried to crowd them out. Of course, there had been barbecues since then, and differences (apart from a fist-fight here and there) managed to be forgotten. But the landowners and their men had gotten vicious of late and must be watched closely like cantankerous dogs. Also the smallholders, in the growing strength of their Association, were more aggressive, not so prone to take gibes from cowboys, more willing to show them exactly where they stood. The peace-loving older townsmen, whose honour and pleasure it was to run the barbecue, were a little uneasy.

The morning came bright and clear, with no promise of the clammy wetness which had turned Main Street into a quagmire a few days before. The meadow was just right, lush and soft to the feet, and men were up at dawn putting the finishing touch to the marquees and stalls, tacking up the banners, the bills and pronouncement, which had been printed by Mowbree's Press.

By ten o'clock yellow-head beanpole Luke Sands with his cripple foot had taken his seat in the little pay-box at a corner of the huge roped area. If he looked to the right he could see the snake-like length of Trinity Valley's Main Street. If he looked the other way he could see the rolling range, the narrow trail, the cluster of little farms and spreads. Further on, where his eyes could not see, the main trail branched off into a myriad spidery little ones, leading to the domains of the Silver Star, the Lame W, the Circle 6.

Coming to him on the breeze came

the sounds of squeaky music as the band warmed up on their rostrum in the cleared space in the centre of the grounds.

The kids came first. For them the admission was only five cents, and all the younger ones received a pat on the head from Luke. He was 'Uncle Luke' to very many of them for he had a batch of comely sisters, each with their own little brood; and, because he had lived in Trinity Valley since he was a boy, a host of friends, whose children too loved the gangling, yellow-haired kindly cripple-man, and called him 'Uncle.'

With the afternoon things really began to hum. The store-keepers who had closed early, and their employees, and cowboys who could manage to make it, streamed into the ground to sample the sideshows. Fat, deep-voiced Widow Murphy, mother of the three fighting brothers, relieved Luke at the pay-box for the latter part of the afternoon, but as dark fell Luke was there again, boisterously cheerful, but apprehensive, for with dusk, recklessness might descend also.

The ground was festooned with lanterns and naphtha flares. The moon came out and the stars. It was a good night. The townsfolk began to make their appearance. John Mowbree and Doctor Billings, both of whom had been bustling around all day, had been home and changed into their best duds; Sheriff Hosell and Deputy Lew Connors, together with a retinue of 'specials' to look after the 'drunks' (and Luke hoped merry drunks would be the only trouble); Sam Garner and a bunch of his pals; the three Murphy brothers; girls from the sporting houses with their slicked-up escorts . . . and so the stream went on.

Already the dancing was under way and Luke could hear the barker calling the turns. His resounding voice rang above all the spieling of the sideshow men, many of them hired specially for the occasion.

'One-two an' a turn around. A kick o' the heels an' a bob to the ground.'

That was a new routine to Luke. He figured that as soon as Ma Murphy showed up again he'd go and have himself a looksee at some of that stuff.

A smart two-horse gig clattered to a stop outside the paybox. Brad Simmons got down and handed the reins to one of the horse-boys. Then he helped his companion down. It was Sally Mowbree: she had kept her promise. Luke Sands frowned. He was a tolerant man, but he did not like what he saw. Many more would like it less. Luke thought about Pat Murphy, and shaking his head slightly, he became a very worried man. He only hoped that Pat would forget his grievance for a bit, and control his temper.

Brad Simmons paid his dues without comment and led his fair companion into the grounds. A few seconds later they had joined the dancers.

Pat and his two brothers were over at the huge punchbowl taking a drink. It was Sol who first noticed the couple. He nudged Manny. Then both of them realized that Pat had seen the couple too. His face had hardened but his eyes hooded his thoughts. He did not say anything but moved away from his two brothers, moved around the edge of the dance-clearing.

'Watch him,' hissed Sol. 'We dassent follow him. Jest watch him that's all.'

Pat moved slowly, a glass of punch untasted in his hand. His eyes were on Sally. She was dressed in a long flowing gown of wine-coloured silk which brought out the full glossy beauty of her golden-brown hair, the soft bloom of her cheeks, the sparkle of her eyes. The gown was plain but daringly low-cut, and there were jewels in her hair which Pat knew had been her mother's. That was something that passed through his mind with everything else, then it was gone, Sally was gone: his eyes were fixed on the man with her.

Brad Simmons had the reputation of being the best dressed man in Trinity

Valley, and right now he was living up to it. His cream-coloured Stetson was slung from its lanyard and hung on his back. He had not checked it in with his gun like most of the boys because it was part of his ensemble. It matched his cream silk shirt with the fancy red markings and the doe-skin gloves he wore. His belt was chased in silver, and his pants were the finest navy-blue velveteen with red piping. His short fancy boots were low-heeled for dancing. His flowing blond hair curled crisply in the nape of his neck and around his ears, and had a golden sheen in the light. Brad was a fine handsome specimen of male humanity. And he could dance too!

The square-dance finished and was followed almost immediately by a waltz. Brad and Sally moved together. They were a perfect pair. Now, by all traditions, the old waltz is an 'excuse-me' dance, and in this fact Pat Murphy saw his chance. He moved in among the dancers. His two brothers watched him. Sol started forward, but Manny halted him with a hand on his arm.

'Let him go,' he said. 'There ain't nothin' we can do.'

'Begob, if he breaks up this party I'll break his fool neck,' said Sol.

Pat reached his objective. He gripped Brad Simmons below the elbow. The blond-haired man turned.

'Excuse me, pardner,' said Pat mildly.

Simmons flushed a little, his hands dropped instinctively. Pat moved smoothly in front of him and took Sally in his arms. They danced away, leaving Brad standing. On the edge of the crowd Sol and Manny heaved huge sighs of relief.

'Yeah, but there's still a good many hours to go,' said Sol gloomily.

Sally Mowbee looked up into Pat's face and mocked him with her eyes. He glowered down at her and said: 'So you came with him after all?'

'I told you I should. I couldn't break my promise.' Her bantering tone left her suddenly. 'You won't start anything here will you, Pat?'

'I ain't makin' any promises,' said the young man truculently.

'Pat — you challenged Brad, didn't you?'

'I did.'

'You didn't mean it. You just lost your temper.'

'I meant it all right. He's been riding for a fall a long time. Him an' his kind want teaching a lesson.'

'So you'd kill him to teach him a lesson?'

'Have you thought that maybe he'd kill me? Still, I guess that wouldn't bother you none.' The man's voice was suddenly bitter.

'Don't talk that way, Pat. I just don't think it's the best way to solve our problems that's all.'

'You think hobnobbing with these people is better maybe . . . '

'You've never tried it.'

'No, and I don't aim to.'

'You're impossible,' she said with a sudden burst of temper.

'I ain't no fancy-man.' Pat's voice was sneering and rough.

Sally lost her patience and pulled away from him on the edge of the floor as the end of the dance came. She flounced away and left him standing.

As she did so she realized it was the wrong thing to do. But by then it was too late and pride forbade her to turn back. A few oldsters and their wives gave Pat sympathetic looks. They had watched all that had happened. They didn't like Brad Simmons either, but their sympathy was the last straw. Pat's face was hot as he turned away from them. He walked blindly to the table which held the drinks and elbowed his way to the front.

His two brothers joined him. 'Don't start any trouble here,' said Sol.

'Mind your own damn' business,' Pat told him.

'Why, yuh young coxcomb, I've a good mind to take yuh out an' give yuh a latherin' me own self.'

Pat swung around viciously. Manny

interposed his solid body between the two of them. Sullenly they subsided. By way of creating a diversion Manny said, 'Look, here come the big bugs.'

Into the barbecue-holdings came Jasper Hart and his painted and hennaed wife, an arrogant Easterner; fat Bill Runshon and his spouse, and Curly Billock, who was a widower, with his only son, a youth called George.

The latter four people were not lacking in common courtesy, though they were sworn enemies of the homesteaders, they greeted people right and left. But Jasper Hart and his spouse did no such thing except that the good lady nodded her head in a supercilious manner to those of her husband's men who touched their foreheads to her. It was said that this woman had a fortune in jewels, that Jasper with all his riches was hard put to meet her incessant demands, that the two of them were forever quarreling over money — their own servants had heard them time and time again. Little wonder that, with a female leech like her attached to him, he wanted to grab all he could. That was his nature too — to grab — it was evident in his pinched cadaverous face, his mean little eyes, his stiff mincing movements. He and his wife began to dance and they moved like mechanical robots.

'It's the Trinity Valley barbecue, the townsfolks' own shindig,' said Pat Murphy. 'Them folks shouldn't be allowed here.'

'No, nor Brad Simmons, I guess,' said Sol.

It was an unfortunate remark. Manny interposed himself once more for Pat had glared at his brother as if he meant to hit him. Pat pushed him roughly aside and strode away.

The band were playing 'The Lancers' and the dancers were moving up and down. Pat snaked in between Brad Simmons and Sally, took Sally's arm. He grinned at Simmons but the mirth did not reach his eyes. Sally found herself being dragged along by her new partner, grinning faces around them. Then Brad caught up, caught hold of Pat's arm.

'This ain't an excuse-me,' he said.

'Ain't it?' said Pat. He let go of Sally, swung around on his toes and drove his fist into Simmons's belly.

The Silver Star ramrod went 'Ouf' and doubled up. Pat moved on, dragging Sally with him. The incident had only been noticed by those in the immediate vicinity. Sally played along. She did not want a wholesale brawl.

Her blue eyes blazed. 'You black-guard,' she said.

Pat grinned. He kept grinning at her until he saw her lips quirk in answer, her eyes dance merrily. They both lost sight of Brad Simmons. Pat danced with a bouncing verve, exhilarating, though some times a little rough on his partner. He carried the girl along with his exuberance. She was laughing and breathless when the dance finished. They stood on the edge of the crowd and Brad Simmons approached them.

His yellow hair was a little dishevelled, his eyes overbright. The word had passed around, and attention was focused on him. He could not take a thing like that lying down.

'Excuse me, Sally,' said Pat quietly. He began to move away.

'Pat,' said the girl. Then as Brad Simmons passed her she called his name too. Neither of them took any notice.

They were moving away from the lights and some of the men-folk began to move after them. The girl stood irresolute, her forehead crinkled with anxiety, then she followed them.

★　★　★

Pat Murphy passed behind a kiddies' roundabout, which was now dark and shrouded in canvas, and ducked under the rope which was the boundary of the barbecue grounds. He moved a little further in the darkness then stopped and turned.

Brad Simmons came into view, halted a few yards away. He took off his hat and dropped it, brim uppermost, on the ground behind him. He took off his gloves and dropped them into it. He took off his kerchief, wiped his forehead and the palms of his hands with it and dropped that into the hat too. He did all this with calculated leisure and arrogance.

Pat, watching him, knew that the handsome cowboy was trying to get him wild, hoping that he would make a false move. But there was no danger of that now. The Irishman was icy cold, his heart sang within him.

As Brad moved forward other men came behind him, hurrying to form a circle around the contestants. There was no talk. Their feet thudded softly, and swished in the long grass.

Brad adopted a fighting stance. Pat followed suit. He knew that here was no rough brawler like Carmody, but a fit, fast-moving man who knew a bit about the gentle art of self-defence. Pat had heard of his prowess in that line. But the Irishman was undaunted, and in a killing mood. He had checked in his gun the same as everybody else when he entered the barbecue. He would kill this prancing fancy-man with his bare hands.

Brad moved in, hooked with his right. Pat blocked it and received a stinging left full in the mouth. He was just marvelling at a man who feinted with his right in such an unorthodox manner, and staggering from the follow-up blow, when another came from nowhere and hit him in the eye. He spun in the air, he saw the stars, bigger than he had ever seen them before. Then he hit the earth hard with the back of his head.

He rolled on to his stomach and got a mouthful of grass, damp and bitter. From a great distance he heard people shouting, it sounded like they were jeering at him. Out of swirling darkness he began to rise, spitting grass from between his teeth. Then he began to see again and the grass was waving gently below him, a couple of inches from his nose, and his blood was dripping slowly upon it, he could see bright drops in the moonlight. He shook his head to dispel his weakness and the drops fell like bright rain.

He felt his life would ebb away from him if he stayed there like a beaten cur. A gust of murderous passion shook his body and the blood seemed to come in torrents. Then the spasm passed and out of his weakness came strength. He grabbed hold of it and rose, twisting to meet his assailant.

Then Clay Hosell's voice rang out. 'What's goin' on here? Break it up!' And another voice said, 'Let 'em be, sheriff, it's a fair fight.' And Pat kept looking around, looking for Brad Simmons. Then Brad was advancing towards him and everybody was silent.

Then into the silence, silence which seemed to blanket even the noise of the sideshows, the shot came like a sword slashing the night apart. Everybody was transfixed by it. A terrible cry quivered on the air and bedlam came on the heels of it. There were many voices shouting. Then one, nearer than the rest, cried: 'Luke Sands has been shot!'

7

After that Pat Murphy lost sight of Brad Simmons altogether and was running with the rest of them.

Luke was sitting in the gloom of his pay-box with his head on one side as if he had dozed off to sleep. Doctor Billings, with his foot on the step, was leaning in towards him, and behind the doctor, Ma Murphy was standing, sobbing her heart out.

Pat had never seen his mother so put out. Then he remembered that she had helped to bring the cripple Luke into the world, and had cared for him as a child after his mother died. He went to her and put his arm around her ample shoulders.

'He's dead, Pat,' she said. 'He's dead. He never had a chance. I was coming down the hill. I saw it all an' couldn't do nothin'. Two riders in masks. One grabbed the cashbox. Luke went for his shotgun and the other shot him point-blank. I couldn't do nothin', Pat. Nothin' . . . '

He was inarticulate. He patted her as he would a child. He was a little stunned himself, all his hurt forgotten, only a dullness gnawing at him. If Clay Hosell had been at his post this might not have happened. And the sheriff had not been there because he was attending to trouble elsewhere. Trouble started by himself — Patrick Murphy. And Luke was dead. Luke was dead.

Doctor Billings backed away, shaking his head, as the sheriff joined him. 'Keep the women away,' he said.

Simultaneous with his words Luke's head lolled forward and the moonlight shone full upon it. Mrs Murphy gave a little cry and sank her head on to Pat's shoulder. Luke Sands' well-remembered face had gone entirely. The impact of this fact on Pat was like a kick in the stomach, pain more blinding and stunning than from any blow he had received from Brad Simmons. His body trembled, and he felt his mother's arms go around him as if her agony had been overwhelmed by what she understood of his, and she strove to comfort him.

He heard Clay Hosell say, 'Did anybody see anything?' And there was confused talk of masked men. Bridles jingled as horses were mounted. Pat came to himself. He pulled away from his mother saying, 'Go home, Ma, everythin's finished,' and then he was running for his own horse.

Manny and Sol were there before him and they helped him to saddle up. Then the three of them rode hard in the wake of the sheriff and his party. They caught up with them, halted on the crest of a rise. The whole party, bunched together, were listening.

'We thought we heard 'em a minute or two ago,' said the sheriff. 'But now there ain't a sound.'

'They had a good start,' said the deputy.

'We'll split up into two parties,' said Hosell decisively. He looked around him, called men's names. Half of the party ranged themselves with him.

'I'll take this bunch,' he said. 'Lew — you take the rest and go that way. We'll go this . . . The Silver Star ranch buildings are down in the middle, the stick-up men 'ud see the light when they got a bit further on. It's a pretty safe bet that they wouldn't make for there.'

'*I* wouldn't bet on it,' said a savage voice in the crowd.

'I'm runnin' this show,' snarled the sheriff. 'An' I don't want any jackasses with me. Anybody who's in an argufyin' mood can go back to town right now.'

Nobody moved. 'All right,' went on Hosell. 'Let's get movin'. The signal 'ull be three shots — spaced apart.'

'All right,' said Lew Connors and wheeled his horse.

The three Murphy brothers were members of his party. 'Spread out, boys,' said Lew. He was a cocky little jasper but he knew his job. 'Not too far. Make it so you can give a sign to the next man in line if you see anythin' suspicious.'

The men, fourteen in all, strung out in a long line. Pat Murphy found himself at the end. A vague bulk to the left of him was his brother, Manny, on his rawboned nag. To the right of him was just blackness.

It was in this blackness that, a few minutes later, he saw a pin-point of light. He moved his horse a little in the other direction and waved to Manny. He saw his elder brother wave to the next man in line, which proved to be Sol.

The three of them moved cautiously towards the light. The rest of them followed more slowly.

'No bandits 'ud be crazy enough to light a fire in the middle of the range just after they'd pulled a job,' said Sol.

'That ain't no fire,' said Manny.

They got nearer and Pat, who was in front, dismounted from his horse. The others followed suit.

'Watch 'em,' hissed Sol to a man behind. The three of them fanned out a little and crept forward.

The light was steady. Pretty soon it was evident that it came through a crack in the shutters of a cabin. A little cabin sunk in a hollow. The Murphy brothers drew their guns and advanced on it from three sides.

Pat sniffed. He could smell wood-smoke and frying bacon. He met his brothers outside the door. 'Looks like a line-hut to me,' he hissed. 'Guess we've been sold a pup.'

'Maybe,' said Sol truculently. He lifted the latch and swung the door wide.

Two men started to their feet in the lamplight. One of them dived for his gun-belt on the back of a chair.

'Hold it,' rapped Sol.

The two men froze. One of them was Big Carmody, the other a lean ranny called 'Stinger' Malloy.

'What's the big idea?' snarled the

latter. He was a fast-talking gent with a habit of chewing tobacco with rapid movements of his lantern jaws. He spat a quid out as he spoke, and eyed the intruders truculently.

Carmody stood with his mouth half-open. His arm was in a sling. His eyes became fixed on Pat Murphy who, gun in hand, moved into the cabin behind his brother. Manny leaned up against the door-jamb.

It was he who whirled suddenly, saying, 'Come on in, pardner, an' jine the party.'

Another Silver Star man came warily past him, blinking in the lamp-light.

'What's goin' on?' he said. 'What do these jaspers want? I jest bin seeing' to the hosses. I — '

'Shaddap,' snarled Sol Murphy. 'Get back over here with yuh pals.'

Sol was suddenly the boss of the family. His voice rang with authority and menace. He was not often like that but his two brothers, the younger and the elder, never failed to remember such occasions.

Incongruously now, Pat suddenly remembered the first time he had heard Sol speak that way, had seen the killer light in his eyes. Pat had been little more than a kid at the time, and Sol had been away months, maybe years, Pat wasn't quite sure how long. And during that time that grim change had come over him. That was many years ago and most times now he was the old well-remembered Sol. The other night he had killed a man. Right now he looked quite capable of killing another, and the three Silver Star men saw the danger signs and stood before him like three graven images. Behind them the pan of bacon atop the hot stove began to smell pungently as it burnt.

'What are you skunks doin' here?' said Sol. To him all Silver Star folk were skunks.

'Whadda yuh think we're doin'?' said Stinger Malloy. 'This is a line hut ain't it? We're on the night turn. Whadda yuh mean bustin' in here like this? What — '

'I'll ask the questions,' said Sol. He gave a significant jerk of his gun. Stinger shut up.

Sol went on: 'Three of yuh in one line hut. That's kind of a crowd aint it?'

'It ain't my turn by rights,' said Stinger, willing to air his grievance even at a time like this. 'It's Jonesy's an' Carmody's. Simmons sent me along 'cos Carmody ain't in good shape.'

'Did Simmons know you were gonna leave here an' make a sudden trip to the barbecue?'

'Barbecue?' If the man's surprise was feigned it was a good piece of acting.

'We ain't bin to no barbeque,' said Carmody. The third man remained silent.

Sol jerked a thumb in his direction. 'He was fixing the hosses, wasn't he? You've been ridin'.'

'We ain't,' said Carmody.

'We've bin scoutin' along the line,' said Stinger Malloy. Both voices spoke almost simultaneously.

'Make up your minds,' said Sol.

'He ain't bin out,' said Stinger quickly. 'Only me an' Jonesy.'

'I'll have a look at the hosses,' said Manny. Pat took his place at the door.

More men were approaching. Lew Connors amongst them. The little deputy moved into the cabin.

'These men admit to have just been ridin',' said Sol.

'What's goin' on?' said Stinger Malloy shrilly. 'What are you after?'

'A man was killed at the barbecue tonight,' said Connors. 'An' the takings stolen by two masked men.'

'We don't know nothin' about that. We've — '

'Lemme see your guns,' said the deputy. 'No funny moves — the place is surrounded with men.'

Only Jonesy still wore his gun. He drew it and handed it over. Gun-belts belonging to Carmody and Malloy were slung over the backs of chairs.

Connors spun the chambers of all three of them, sniffed at the muzzles.

He looked up from the last one. 'Whose is this?' he said.

'That's Malloy's,' said Carmody.

'All right,' snarled the lean man, turning on him. 'I ain't denyin' it am I?'

'It's bin fired recently,' said Connors.

'I took a pot at a coyote about'n hour ago.'

'You did, uh?'

At this juncture Manny Murphy returned. 'Two o' them hosses've been ridden purty hard,' he said. 'They're still blowin' a little although they've bin watered an' fed.'

'I told yuh, we rode along the line,' said Malloy. 'We gave 'em their head comin' back.'

'Search the place,' said Connors. 'A couple of yuh look around by them hosses.'

Men began to spread out across the cabin. The burning bacon began to smoke. A man threw it outside, pan and all.

'You cain't do this,' protested Malloy. 'This is Silver Star property — '

111

'Shaddap,' Sol Murphy told them again. 'Get over in that corner the three of yuh. Keep still an' keep quiet.' The posse turned the place upside down and searched the hollow all around it, moving up on to the slopes and among the stunted scrub, but they did not find a single cent of the pile of money they sought. However, Connors decided to take the three men in for questioning. The recently fired gun, the blown horses, were very suspicious items.

'You said there was on'y two men,' complained big Carmody petulently. 'An' my hoss ain't bin rode.'

'You kin ride him now,' said Connors.

The cavalcade moved away from the now darkened cabin. After a short interval Connors said, 'I guess we'd better give the signal.' He raised his gun in the air and fired three shots.

After a moment there were three answering ones. 'Burn the wind,' said the little deputy and set his horse at a faster pace. The three prisoners, tied to lead ropes, were bounced about on their horses' backs.

When Connors' party came up with the other one it was evident that they, too, had struck oil. The whole bunch of them were dismounted from their horses and gathered amid a clump of trees. They stood in a circle around a man who sat on the ground in a huddle of blankets.

'You go to bed kinda early, don't yuh, stranger?' Sheriff Hosell was saying.

A drawling voice with a harsh undertone replied, 'I go to bed when I'm tired, pardner. I was tired early tonight.'

'You bin ridin' hard I guess.'

'No more'n usual I guess. I was jest plumb tired.'

That drawling half-mocking voice with the bitter underlying harshness struck a chord in Pat Murphy's memory. He remembered the stranger he had met on the hill the back of town the other night. And, on moving nearer he discovered it was indeed that man.

'You ain't answered my questions,' said Hosell.

'I was half asleep when you jumped me. I didn't hear your blamed questions.'

'You were that much half asleep that you'd got your gun in your hand. You'd've plugged me I guess if you hadn't seen I had company.'

'I might at that. You asked for it bustin' in on a man while he's trying to get a quiet spell of shut-eye.'

Pat Murphy listened intently for the stranger's reply. He was thinking it had taken the man a hell of a long time to get such a short ride away from the town. He was still in Trinity Valley actually, and probably on Silver Star land. The man took his time in answering. Finally he said: 'So that's why you're runnin' around an' pouncin' on folks in the dark, uh? What am I supposed to do about the man who's been killed an' the money that's been stolen?'

'Maybe the question is what *have* you

done about it,' said Clay Hosell.

The stranger had nothing to say to this so the sheriff continued: 'Where yuh bound for?'

'No place in particular.'

'We ain't seen yuh in town.'

'What town's that?'

'I'll ask the questions. There's only one town near here.'

'I guess that 'ud be the little burg I passed the back of the other night. I didn't figger it was worth takin' a look in on.' The stranger's tone was infuriating.

One of the posse suggested the sheriff should kick his teeth in. Hosell did not take the advice, but barked: 'Stand up!'

He followed the words with an upward jerk of the Colt in his hand and slowly the stranger rose. He was tall and dark-garbed and rangy.

'I'm the sheriff o' this territory,' said Hosell. 'An' when I ask questions I like 'em answered properly. If you ain't done no harm nobody's gonna hurt yuh. You ain't helping yourself none by trying to be smart.'

'I'm a solitary kind of hairpin. I like to hear myself talk sometimes,' said the other.

'Talk properly then. Who are yuh? Where'd yuh come from?'

'The name of a saddle-tramp like me wouldn't be of interest to folks. Last place I was in was Tombstone.'

'What did yuh do in Tombstone?'

'Jest lounged I guess.'

The sheriff opened his mouth to speak again but was forestalled by the appearance of one of his men, who said, 'His hoss ain't bin ridden hard.'

'I never ride my hoss hard.'

'Where's your pard?' shot out the sheriff.

The man hesitated again before he spoke. Then he said, 'So there was two men in on this shootin' was there? Wal, I'm sorry to disappoint yuh but, like I told yuh before, I'm a solitary man. I ain't got no pard.'

The sheriff took his gun and examined it. 'I'd like it back when

116

you've finished,' said the stranger. Hosell handed it back without comment.

'Search his baggage an' all around,' he said. He turned and joined his deputy, heard his tale and had a look at the other three prisoners.

The tall stranger looked on without comment while the posse ransacked his belongings and sniffed and trampled the ground all around like a lot of busy gophers. They found nothing of a suspicious nature; in fact, the stranger was travelling very light.

The sheriff said: 'I'll hafta take you in for questioning. You're a damsight too reticent f'r my likin'.'

'I was under the impression we'd had quite an agreeable discussion,' said the other in his slow, harsh, mocking voice. The sheriff snorted.

'Git on your hoss,' he said.

The stranger looked around him at the menacing silent men, many of them with drawn guns. He shrugged broad slopping shoulders, the shoulders of a fighter, a gun hawk. He said: 'Who am I to argue with such crushing persuasion. I shall be honoured to take advantage of your hospitality, and pursue our discussion further.'

'Lemme shut him up, Clay,' growled Lew Connors, moving forward with gun swinging.

The stranger stiffened. 'Get away from me, little man,' he said.

'Quit it, Lew,' rapped the sheriff.

The little deputy danced on his toes like a terrier. But he looked back at the sheriff then came away.

The stranger turned his back, bent it, and began to gather his stuff together. He stashed everything in his bed-roll and tied it to the back of his saddle. Then he mounted. One of the posse started forward with a rope.

'Don't crowd me,' said the stranger.

'Let him be,' said the sheriff.

The formation moved off. Stinger Malloy, Carmody and Jonesy could be heard grumbling in the rear.

A lean homesteader, who had had

a couple of haystacks mysteriously burned a week ago, raised his rifle and told them to 'Stow it before he cracked 'em one.'

The cavalcade reached the now deserted site of the barbecue. A few flares flickered here and there, like pale ghosts of the festivities. They seemed to speak of the tragedy that had ended everything far more eloquently than total darkness would have done.

The prisoners were strangely silent. Maybe they too felt something, something maybe of the savage thoughts which filled the minds of their captors.

They passed by an archway which, an hour ago had been festooned with lanterns and a man said, with the high harshness of hysteria, 'I vote we string 'em up there right now.'

'Talk sense — or shut your trap altogether,' snarled the sheriff.

A few moments later the silent party rode into the main drag of Trinity Valley. The townsfolk streamed out to meet them and pandemonium broke loose. Questions were yelled from all sides, many folks tried to get at the prisoners.

'Make way,' bawled Clay Hosell. 'Have you all gone crazy?'

Jack Carless, barman, who had lived in Abilene in its heyday and met all the great ones, came out on to the stoop of the Proud Valley Saloon. He saw the tall stranger riding beside Sheriff Clay Hosell and said: 'Jumpin' Jesophat — John Harding!'

The news spread like a forest fire. In an hour's time all the town knew that the sheriff had the notorious gunman in jail, along with three Silver Star men. The four men were connected by wildly wagging tongues. It was said that Jasper Hart had hired John Harding to do his killings for him.

8

Despite everything, Pat Murphy discovered that he had taken a liking to the tall gunslinger. The news that he was John Harding gave him little surprise. There was something about the man that stamped him out of the ordinary.

Something about his drawling, mocking voice with that harsh, almost bitter undertone. Something about the way he carried himself, the slope of his shoulders; the hang of his long arms; the angle of his gunbelt with the holster well forward; the lean brooding look of his face; the hooded eyes; the mocking quirk of the lips which had in it very little mirth — maybe only a deep cynicism.

Pat knew the man had nothing to do with Malloy and Carmody and Jonesy. Or at least, he hoped he knew. He told his brothers of how he had met the man outside town a few nights previous.

'Maybe I ought to tell the sheriff,' he said.

'Tell the sheriff nothin',' said brother Sol shortly.

Pat bridled at his tone. 'I'll tell him if I want to. I don't need any advice from you,' he said, although he had already decided not to tell Hosell anything. He liked Hosell, he was a good lawman; but Pat, being a fighting Irishman, was congenitally opposed to authority.

The following morning Judge Lynus's handsome equipage, with the top-hatted negro, Mose, seated erect on the box, rolled along Main Street and drew to a stop outside the sheriff's office and jail. The old man got down and entered the former. It was a practise of his to look important new prisoners over and, oftimes, harangue them.

He was in there for about an hour and all that time Mose sat erect on his seat like a graven ebony image, ignoring the stares of passersby and the jibes of small boys. Observation was kept on the point by barflies, shopkeepers, and loungers, from the windows of the Proud Valley and other nearby establishments, and finally the judge was seen to resume his position. His carriage rolled away. The front of the office remained blank and uncommunicative.

About half an hour later John Harding walked through the door into the sunshine, and the town came alive with a bang like a mule with a firecracker under its tail.

The notorious gunman paused on the boardwalk and looked about him. He wore his gun, and his bedroll was under his arm. Finally he tipped his hat to the back of his head, turned sharply left, and began to walk, but his head was not still, his eyes raked everywhere around him. Folks stepped off the sidewalk to let him pass and eyed him sullenly or with simple interest. Heads vanished from windows as if they had been pulled by strings.

Folks in the Proud Valley heard his boot-heels thudding. Then the sound stopped. Then the batwings swung open and he came in. He looked around him as any man would on entering a strange place. There was nothing truculent about his gaze — but no interest either. He went to the bar and ordered whiskey.

At a table sat 'Sudsy' Porter. Sudsy would have little part in any well-told tale. He was a no-good, a small-time grafter, a braggart and a sot. He was insignificant; and because, in his heart, he was aware of that fact, he flaunted his toughness and little meannesses like banners of glory.

He had been talking loudly about how they ought to string those killers up higher than kites, and drinking himself into a slobbering rage. Then Harding came in and a man next to Sudsy said: 'There's one of 'em, why don't you tell him?'

'I will,' said Sudsy. 'I will.' He drained his glass with a gulp.

Another man said: 'That's John Harding. You don't say things to him. He'll blow your haid off. He killed two men in Tombstone. You've heard o' John Harding, ain't yuh, Sudsy? You've heard of John Harding ain't yuh?'

The man's jeering voice needed an answer. Sudsy said, 'Sure I've heard of John Harding. He's just a cheap gunny.'

'Keep your voice low f'r Pete's sake,' said the first man.

'Sudsy ain't scared o' no li'l ol' John Hardin', air yuh, Sudsy?' said the second.

'What you tryin' to do, Clem?' said the first. 'Get Sudsy kilt?'

Sudsy said: 'Naw, I ain't scared o' no cheap gunny.' His voice was becoming more penetrating.

The tall man by the bar sipped his drink and looked into nothingness. He did not seem to notice the way folks sidled away from him, the way the seedy-looking man with the red unshaven face spoke in a loud voice.

'Why ain't he in jail with his three

125

murderin' pards?' said Sudsy. 'Why ain't he in jail, I say!'

This time his voice was plain enough for everybody to hear. Heads were turned in his direction, eyes covertly watched John Harding, people shifted again. Nobody answered Sudsy's question. 'Cut it out, will yah!' said the drunkard's well-wishing companion. The other man, who had egged him on, was now silent. He realized that maybe he had gone too far: anything could happen with a drunken coot like Sudsy, who thought he was tough.

The notorious gunman still did not make any sign. He reached for the bottle at his elbow and everybody, including Sudsy, stiffened. But Harding merely poured himself a drink.

Sudsy was heartened. This tall nonchalant-looking gink was just a flash in the pan, a sharpshooter who had killed a few men and was trading on his reputation as a killer. Bluff was his strong point. That's all he was doing now, standing there and trying to bluff everybody. But not Sudsy Porter, no, sir, Sudsy was the bad man of Trinity Valley, he seen them come and he had seen them go. He'd show this smart Alec where he got off and, if he got tough, why, he'd plug him clean between the eyes. He'd go down in history as the man who killed John Harding, the fastest gun in the West. Fastest gun, pah! — he'd show them who was the fastest gun!

He gave a hitch to his belt and lurched to his feet. 'I want 'nother drink,' he said.

'Watch yourself, Sudsy,' said his companion and moved his own chair back to the wall out of the line of fire.

Sudsy swaggered up to the bar and banged it with his fist. He stood a few yards away from John Harding.

Jack Carless ran up. 'Don't start any trouble in here,' he said. 'Unless you want to get pitched out on your ear . . . Take no notice of this half-wit, Mr Harding,' he said — aside.

The truculence of the barman was a set-back for Sudsy. He was knocked off-balance for a moment. Finally he decided to ignore this small fry. 'Gimme a drink,' he said.

Carless eyed him for a moment then passed a bottle across the bar. Sudsy took it, poured some into his glass, slopped a little on to the bar. Carless continued to watch him for a moment then, as if satisfied that he had quietened down, turned away and went along to the other end of the bar. The saloon was very quiet. Sudsy emptied his glass with a gulp. Then he leaned one elbow on the bar and looked at John Harding.

The tall man seemed to become suddenly aware that he was being stared at. He turned and looked at Sudsy.

Sudsy said: 'Why ain't you in jail?'

'You addressing me, pardner?'

'I am.'

'The name's Harding.'

'Yeah, I know that. Why've they let

you outa jail, *Mister* Harding?'

Harding did not answer right off. He merely slid along the bar towards Sudsy. The latter started a little then, when he realized the notorious gunman wasn't making any funny moves, stood his ground. Gosh, this so-called badman was a pushover.

'Wal, I'll tell yuh, pardner,' said Harding mildly. 'Me an' the ol' jedge an' the sheriff, we had a little palaver, an' we decided that there was nothin' I could be held for. I ain't shot nobody since Tombstone — I never shoot folks without givin' 'em an even break — an' I ain't got a red cent 'cept my own dirty little roll of bills.'

Sudsy blinked owlishly, a little nonplussed by this naïve reply. Somebody tittered. That did it.

Sudsy, a sudden contemptuous anger against this man surging up inside of him, really took the bull by the horns. 'Horsefeathers!' he sneered harshly. 'You shot Luke Sands. You gotta be hanged for it.'

John Harding smiled. 'Who did you say I shot, pardner?'

Sudsy's jaw dropped. His hand went automatically to his belt. John Harding moved a little closer.

Panic struggled with rage in Sudsy's drink-sodden mind. He was being hazed by this tall smiling buzzard. He backed away.

'You might fool other people with your fancy reputation but you don't get past me!' he screeched and went for his gun.

There was a flash, a deafening explosion; Sudsy screeched again and staggered back. His gun did a buck and wing across the bar-room floor and came to rest finally, a mangled piece of metal, beneath a table.

John Harding sheathed his gun and moved forward again. 'Ain't many men can do that, pardner,' he said. 'Many a man would have blown your haid off.' Then his voice changed, it rasped gratingly.

'In every tinpot town I come to I see

worms like you. They come crawling from under their rocks to look at me. Then they try to bite me. I hafta squash 'em.'

This was worse than death. This was the crowning humiliation. As the tall man came on Sudsy saw the contempt in his eyes, and he nursed his tingling hand and tried to spit again like a cat at bay. Then John Harding reached out and gave him a stinging smack across the face. He fell on his backside against the wall and sat there. He watched the tall man stride across the room and through the batwings. Then he got up and slunk away.

John Harding went to the livery-stables and got his horse. After that he passed from the ken of the people of Trinity Valley. All except one of them. Could the rest have seen an incident that happened that night it would have set them wondering.

★   ★   ★

131

As Sol Murphy came out of his mother's house he whirled at the approach of a tall man from the shadows. Then he relaxed. He held out his hand and John Harding gripped it and said: 'I couldn't leave without saying so-long.'

'Have you seen anybody else, John?'

'No, nobody came to see me in jail — so, I thought it was better this way.'

'Nobody had much chance, John.'

'Mebbe not. But I still think it's better this way.'

'I didn't tell the folks who you were.'

'I know, thank you for keeping quiet.'

'It didn't do much good. I forgot Jack Carless claimed to know yuh. Evidently he told the truth.'

'Somebody allus knows me,' said Harding half to himself. 'Thanks anyway, Sol.'

'You don't hafta thank me for anythin', John. Not since that night in Waco, remember, when we tried to hold up Wells Fargo. That long-haired galoot sure had the drop on me. I'd've been for the Happy Huntin' Grounds if you hadn't slugged him.'

'That seems a hell of a long time ago, Sol.'

'Yeah, it's a long time.'

'I ought to have stopped then the same as you did. But I didn't, I went on. An' what's it got me? The fastest gun in the West!' He gave a little spurt of harsh laughter.

'Come in an' meet the folks, John. Come on in an' surprise 'em.'

'No thanks, Sol. I ain't no surprise package. I'll get moving.' There was an air of finality about this pronouncement. He held out his hand.

Sol grasped it and shook it again. Neither man said anything more. Harding turned about. Sol watched him until he disappeared into the gloom, then he went on through the alley to the main street.

9

There was a rumour flying around that Sheriff Hosell had been to the Silver Star Ranch to make certain enquiries, that Jasper Hart had refused to see him and that he and his posse had been driven from the spread by armed men. Then that night Brad Simmons rode into town, dismounted outside the sheriff's office and went inside.

He was not in there long, and when he came out he looked hopping mad. He went straight to the Proud Valley and up to the bar. Then he asked if anybody had seen that yellow Irish skunk, Pat Murphy. The gauntlet was tossed back with a vengeance. The news passed from lip to lip with sensational rapidity.

Some time later young Sam Garner ran into the print-shop where Sally and her father were still working. He stopped, panting, until old John made his usual query.

'What's bitin' you, Sam?'

Then the youth burst out with the news. 'Brad Simmons is in the Proud Valley waitin' for Pat Murphy. Pat's on his way down there now.'

'Oh, the fools,' cried Sally. 'The fools!'

She tore off her apron and donned her short coat. Then she made for the door.

'Sally,' called her father. The bang of the door was the only reply he received.

'Go with her, Sam,' he said, and as the youth darted away, took off his own apron and put on his coat.

When he got outside he could not see the girl or the youth. In a shuffling run he made for the Proud Valley. He was not the only one going in that direction.

As Sally and Sam ran down the street they saw Pat Murphy. The girl called his name. If he heard the cry he did not heed it. He was walking with short sharp steps on his high-heeled boots, covering the ground at a tremendous rate. Sally began to run faster so that even the lanky Sam was hard put to keep up with her. Men fanned out on the boardwalk as Pat climbed the stoop before the saloon. He went through the batwings. The girl raced after him.

'You can't go in there, Miss Sally,' said one of the men, and tried to bar her way. She pushed him, and he staggered from the fury of her attack. Then she was past him and through the doors.

Pat had halted in the centre of a cleared space. Brad Simmons moved forward slowly towards him, half-crouching, his hand clawed a few inches above the butt of his gun.

'Stop it,' cried Sally. She flung herself forward and grasped Pat's arm.

He tried to shake her off. Brad Simmons drew his gun and fired.

'The girl!' shouted somebody.

Pat had flung her away from him. Two men had grabbed hold of Simmons and were holding him. There were angry cries.

Pat staggered. Blood streamed from his arm. Sally put her arms around his shoulders and her eyes blazed at Simmons, who struggled impotently with those who held him.

'You coward,' she said. 'You sly, filthy coward. I ought to have let him kill you.'

Simmons's face changed. 'I didn't see you, Sally,' he said. 'I didn't realize — '

'You're a liar,' she spat at him. 'You saw the chance to get the drop on Pat and you took it.'

'What shall we do with him, Miss Sally?' said one of the men.

The girl's voice dripped with contempt. 'Just let him go.'

Simmons's manner underwent another transformation.

'You'll pay for this — all of yuh,' he said. He looked at the girl as he passed her and, although he did not speak, his eyes were full of hate.

His handsome face was contorted with it, and Sally wondered what she had ever seen in him. Why had she thought him such an amusing companion. Amusing? Why, he was like a coyote showing its fangs.

Pat pulled away from her. 'I've still got another arm, Simmons,' he said.

'Let him go, Pat,' she said. 'Let him go.' Others joined with her in this plea.

Simmons did not turn around. The batwings swung to behind him.

Pat dropped into a chair. Sally gently rolled up his sleeve. Something he saw glowing softly in her eyes made him suddenly ashamed. The hate in him died quickly, he wanted to tell the world how happy he was.

The wound was a mere flea-bite, a long groove in his left upper-arm. The sharp-shooting Simmons had been too hasty. Jack Carless brought bandages and salve, and there and then Sally bandaged the arm up. Her father and Sam Garner stood nearby and watched. Neither of them said anything. It was doubtful whether either the man or the girl would have heard them if they had spoken. They seemed to be in a little world of their own.

Afterwards they went outside together and moved towards Pat's home. Old John and young Sam watched them go. Then the former said: 'Come on, younker, we've got work to do.'

As they moved down the street Sheriff Hosell came riding in with a small posse. The big lawman left his horse with the livery-boy and fell into step with the printer and his assistant.

'Find anything, Clay?' said John.

'Not a thing. We've been over that cabin again like a herd o' bugs — an' hunted all around it. An' tried every hidin' place we know for miles around. That money must be buried mighty deep. Either that or we've got the wrong men. Maybe the two men who took it are in another state by now.'

'Is that your real opinion, Clay?'

'Hell,' snorted the sheriff. 'I'm that thrown an' hog-tied I don't even know what my own opinion is any more.' He reflected for a moment and John wisely left him to it.

Then the lawman said: 'I'm still mighty suspicious about them three Silver Star men. The blown horses — Malloy's gun, which had recently been fired — the fact that there was three line-riders 'stead o' the usual one or two, as if Carmody was kept for look-out. One thing in itself wouldn't be so suspicious, but the 'ull three add up to something mighty fishy. An' the ol' jedge agrees with me. What do you think, John?'

'I'm inclined to agree with you both,' said the printer. Then he added tentatively. 'Do you think the money's hidden, maybe, at the Silver Star ranch-house?'

'I had thought of that. That's one reason I went there. You've heard about the reception I got. The trouble is that although I'm holding three of his men, I ain't got no rights at all to rampage across Jasper Hart's holdings — an' the mealy-mouthed skunk knows it.'

'Maybe after all this you'll be more in favour of the Cattlemens' Association,' said the printer.

'For Pete's sake don't bring that up now,' said the sheriff.

Old John's dogmatism could be very irritating at times. He stiffened and Hosell expected a hot retort. But the old man simmered down, and when he spoke again his voice was quite level.

'The three men could have had another accomplice to whom they passed the money.'

'Yeh, I'd thought of that. But who? Not Harding.'

'No, I think Harding's in the clear.'

'Then it could have been another Silver Star man. An' there's dozens of 'em.'

'A lot of 'em were at the barbecue.'

'All right, maybe I'd better find out who wasn't there. An' maybe I ought to get the judge to make me out a search-warrant to go over the Silver Star from top to bottom. That'd probably start the wholesale range war

I've been trying to avoid all this time.'

'Is the judge going to try the three men in the near future?'

'If he does he can't find them guilty of murder on such circumstantial evidence. We've got to find that money. I'm keeping them three tight in jail for the time being. Jasper Hart can send all his smart lawyers — an' be damned to him.'

'Brad Simmons was at your office while you were out,' said John.

'He was, was he? Wantin' to know all the whys an' wherefors I guess. I reckon Lew sent him away with a flea in his ear.'

'It certainly looked that way.' Old John went on to tell the lawman of the incident in the saloon. When he had finished Hosell was silent for a moment. Then he said: 'It was a bad thing, John — but I guess them two young hellions 'ud bin boilin' up to it for a long time. It was a plucky thing your gel did. She might've bin killed.'

'She's headstrong. But she certainly

knew what she meant to do that time.'

'She certainly picked a headstrong one to match in Pat Murphy.'

Both old stagers nodded their heads sagely. Then the sheriff pulled himself up. What was he doing — doddering in his old age?

'If Pat Murphy don't get a holt of himself I'll clap him in jail to cool him off,' he said.

After asserting himself in this forthright manner the sheriff of Trinity Valley took his leave, and the press-men carried on to their work.

★ ★ ★

The following day things were pretty quiet in the little township. There were no more visits from the Silver Star men. An occasional Lame W and Circle 6 ranny rode in to pick up supplies and, after a drink in the saloon, where they were regaled by Jack Carless with the doings of the previous day, they drifted out again.

Sudsy Porter was skulking in his hovel at the edge of town, scared to show his face after his humiliation. Folks still talked about that incident, hoping to see the legendary John Harding once more. But he did not put in an appearance. Pat Murphy did not come around to receive congratulations on his lucky escape after the treachery of that snake, Simmons, but about noon his brother Sol began tacking up bills all around the place. At each one little knots of men and women gathered. It was, as they had expected, another Cattlemens' Association pronouncement.

There was to be a meeting in the Proud Valley Saloon at eight o'clock that evening. The subject would be the 'cutting-out' of land for nesters and homesteaders. That meant, according to most peoples' speculations, that each man should slice off as much as he needed and fence it in — not to isolate himself from his neighbours, but from the land of the big ranches. But who was to say where the acres of the Silver Star, Circle 6 and Lame W ended? They had their own tentative dividing lines between each spread, but as far as they were concerned the settlers who scratched a living on the outskirts and, who in law had as much rights to the land as they, had no holdings whatsoever. Hence their frequent encroachments, such as driving cattle across crops, pulling down haystacks, fouling water.

The use of fences had been suggested before but, on these rolling plains, even the smallest 'nesters' shrank from their use. There was much speculation and not a little arguing. The general opinion now was, whether they liked fences or not, their use seemed to be the only way of stopping the encroachment of the 'big bugs'. The hide-bound argument against that was, of course, that fences did not mean a thing to a herd of cattle.

'The fences won't be just fences,' said a philosophical old-timer. 'They'll be a kind of a symbol. They'll show them skunks we mean business, that our little bit o' land means as much to us as all the acres o' theirs. They ain't paid for any of it no more than we have, we'll take what we want same as they did — Lord knows we ain't askin' for much — an' ef'n they wasn't such damned hogs they wouldn't begrudge us our little bit.'

Another settler, a serious-faced young man, chimed in. 'I think they're just a little bit scared. They think we'll keep on growin' same as they did, and because there's so many of us we'll finish by swallowin' 'em up.'

'Serve 'em damwell right,' said the old-timer, humorously unreasonable. He went on: 'An' if they violate our boundaries we'll fight 'em. If we stick together 'stead o' backbitin' among ourselves there'll be enough of us. That's what I say — fight 'em! Drive 'em out!'

'That'd mean range-war.'

'So? It wouldn't be the first

range-war I've been mixed up in.'

'You're a widower,' said the serious young man. 'You've got three grown-up sons. You haven't got a wife an' three little kiddies same as me. You're talkin' like a lunatic.'

'Lunatic am I? Unwashed mavericks like you 'ud let yourselves be trampled on if it wasn't for old 'uns like me.'

'Don't you believe it, pop,' said another young man. 'If you want to fight I'm with yuh.'

'Ain't much use argufying about it now,' said a sage middle-aged man. 'Best to see what crops up at the meetin'.'

Even at the meeting, however, opinions were very much divided. Many who already had sneaking ambitions of expansion, even while they hotheadedly reviled the landowners for holding that very creed, were chary of fixing their boundaries with fences. Others went to the other extreme and suggested barbed wire. The meeting broke up in disorder. Little knots of men stood on street corners and argued into the small hours. Finally they drifted homewards and Trinity Valley was left to the depradations of prowling cats, and a bold young coyote who paid nightly visits to the garbage cans.

The only glimmer of light came from the print-shop where the industrious John Mowbree was again working late, getting out a bombshell of an edition for the morrow. Finally that light, too, went out.

10

Lew Connors had promised to relieve the sheriff at the jail at two a.m. He left his room at the boarding-house at a quarter to the hour and strolled leisurely down Main Street, keeping to the dusty road so that his footsteps would not resound on the boardwalk.

He was passing a dark alcove, the entrance to Abe Coogan's Saddle Emporium, when he saw a shadow move. He stopped, his hand moving towards his gun.

A voice hissed, 'Lew,' then again, urgently, 'Lew.'

The little deputy kept his hand on his gun-butt and began to move slowly forward. The shadow was still now.

'Who are yuh?' said Lew. 'Come on out of there.'

He was a peppery little gent. He

pranced forward like a terrier smelling a fight.

The voice, which he did not recognize, said, 'It's only me, Lew.'

Lew went a little closer. His hackles rose and he started to pull his gun. Another voice to the side of him said 'Better leave it where it is. Unless you want your haid blown off.'

His hand remained still, he turned slowly. There was another man, he must have been hiding in the shadows. A gun glinted in his fist. Behind him was a third man. Then a footfall behind Lew made him turn again. Yet another man was advancing from another direction. He was surrounded by them.

The man who had first spoken came out of the doorway. His face was covered by a dark kerchief, his hat pulled low over his eyes.

'Turn around, Lew,' he said huskily.

'What's the idea?'

'Do as you're told.'

There was no mistaking the menace in that voice. Lew turned. His gun was whisked neatly out of its holster.

'Now carry on to where you were goin'. Use the side door like you allus do.'

'So you've bin spyin' on me — '

'Shaddap. Get movin'. An' remember we're right behind yuh. One false move an' you'll be riddled like a sieve. Get off the walk. Take it quietly like you were doing before.'

Lew's little wiry body vibrated with anger. But he was no fool. Best to control his feelings, and do as he was told. He halted at the side door of the jail. The men fanned out around him. There were about eight of them and they were all masked. The husky-voiced one who seemed to be the leader spoke again; Lew had the idea he was trying to disguise his voice as he said: 'Knock the door an' tell the sheriff you're here. If you say a miss-word we'll kill yuh an' we'll get the sheriff too eventually. Both of you'll stay healthy if you play your cards right. Go on, knock!'

'I don't know who you are,' said Lew.

'But you won't get away with a thing like this . . . Mebbe I *do* know who you are. You — '

'Knock,' snarled the man. He brought his gun-barrel forward viciously, jabbing the sharp rim hard into the little man's stomach.

Lew gulped in agony. 'Knock,' said the man again. 'I've told you what'll happen if you don't. D'yuh want us to shoot the town up?'

Lew turned, raised his fist and rapped the door. There was silence for a moment, then the sound of footsteps inside.

A subdued voice said. 'That you, Lew?'

The gun jabbed viciously again. Lew said, 'Yeh, it's me, Clay.'

A chain rattled. Then the door began to open.

'Look out, Clay!' cried Lew.

The masked man slashed him across the face with the barrel of the gun, then as he fell leapt over him and threw himself at the door. But the sheriff had not taken the chain away. The door stuck.

The masked man cursed and fired three times. Then he leapt back. There was no answering fire. Only silence. Lew Connors lay still on the ground. The men around him were still.

'Don't stand there,' said the leader. 'Help me to get this door open. I didn't bargain for this. We shall have to work fast. Bull — Jodey — here.'

Two big men came forward and put their shoulders to the door. It creaked and groaned protestingly before the staple of the chain came out of the wall entirely. The door opened slowly. There was still something holding it.

Before passing through the aperature with Bull and Jodey, the leader turned and said: 'Grimes an' Sailor, you fetch the horses. The rest of you stay here. If there's interference you'll hafta start shooting.'

Light streaming through from the passage where the cell-block lay fell on Sheriff Hosell. His eyes were closed.

There was blood on his clothes. He was either dead or very near to it. The two big masked men, with guns drawn, moved warily down the passage. The leader bent over Clay Hosell and took the jail keys from his belt. He ran after the others. A few moments later he had the three prisoners out of their cells. The six men joined the others. The horses were waiting, but already there were sounds of people stirring in the town. The moaning Lew was dragged in beside his boss and the door shut upon them.

The men mounted. 'Let's go,' said the leader.

Even as he spoke the door behind him crashed open. Lew Connors stood swaying there, the sheriff's gun in his hand. His shot took the leader's hat off. Then the latter's gun barked twice. Lew gave a choking cry and pitched forward.

The riders swept on down Main Street. Lights were flashing on. A man shouted. The light went on again at the print-shop, blazing through the shattered windows. John Mowbree had not yet retired. He came running out with his shotgun in his hand. He raised it. The leader of the masked men swerved his horse, deliberately galloping him straight for the old printer. He was firing as he charged. John Mowbree's gun flew from his hands. The old man fell backwards on to the boardwalk. He caught hold of a post and tried to pull himself up. His weakened fingers failed to find a grip. He crumpled and lay still. His daughter ran out of the shop and flung herself on her knees beside him.

★　★　★

Taken by surprise, the people of Trinity Valley were momentarily stunned. Men on horseback, with hastily clutched weapons and in various stages of undress clattered out in pursuit of the attackers. They were a raggle-taggle posse with no lawman to help them. They returned empty-handed. The masked men had had a good start. The posse had not even had a smell of them.

With the dawn the full extent of the stunning tragedy was known. Both old John Mowbree and Lew Connors were dead. Sheriff Hosell was still clinging tenaciously to life, but he remained unconscious, and Doctor Billings said he might never come to himself on this side of the Divide.

The masked men had come, liberated the prisoners and gotten away scot-free without leaving a trace. Clay Hosell was laid up at Ma Murphy's place where Sally Mowbree, too, was a constant visitor. She was bearing up well, but could not be persuaded to leave the rooms above the print-shop where her father lay dead.

The general opinion was that the masked men had been from the Silver Star, come to set their comrades free. No other conclusion seemed possible. Feeling ran high but without their leaders the people were erratic. A raging bunch of settlers rode down on the Silver Star and were suddenly surrounded by men who bristled with arms, and had the drop on them. Their accusations were received with laughter and jeers and they were shepherded away.

Somebody said maybe it was not the Silver Star after all, maybe the three rannies had been working with a bunch from another ranch all along, unknown to Jasper Hart. The settlers were only prevented from making 'sorties' on the other two big ranches by the sudden appearance of Judge Lynus. He said they would accomplish nothing by rampaging around the countryside like that except maybe get themselves killed.

He had no plan, he had nothing to work on, he could only hope that Clay Hosell would regain consciousness and be able to tell them something. So the town simmered and rumbled and waited and hard-faced men scoured the countryside in bunches — to no avail.

* * *

Pat Murphy's wounded arm healed quickly. He spent hours at the bedside of Clay Hosell, looking down at the pale, aquiline face with the raven black hair, resting his head on the broad chest, where life still fluttered, willing the lawman to live, to wake up and talk. Sometimes Sally was there with him. He comforted her with inarticulate gentleness.

The funerals of John Mowbree and Lew Connors were moving affairs, in which the whole town streamed out to pay homage.

The following morning Sally and Pat went riding together. They spoke very little until they were out in the centre of the plains with no signs of humans or habitation in their sight.

Then Pat stopped his horse suddenly and reached out to put his hand tentatively on her arm. He told her he had a question to ask her but she need not give her answer right now, she need not say anything. There and then he said that when all this was over he'd like to marry her, start a little spread of their own. They needn't stay here if she didn't want to, he'd go anywhere she pleased. It was a queer time to ask her he knew, but he wanted her to know how he felt — just in case anything happened, and he didn't have a chance to tell her —

'Don't say that, Pat,' she said. 'Please don't say that. I'll marry you; I'll marry you as soon as you want me to. Dad would have wanted it, I know he would — '

Words failed her then. She turned her horse's head.

They rode back to town.

That afternoon Pat went out with his brothers on another scouting expedition. They went to the line-hut where Malloy, Carmody and Jonesy had been captured. The place was deserted and in disorder.

'A bunch of the boys came here yesterday,' said Sol. 'They ran into some Silver Star men, and didn't have a chance to do what they intended. We'll do it.' He produced a crowbar from his rifle-boot.

They got to work on the floorboards.

'Ol' man Hart 'ull probably sue us if he finds out who's done this,' said Sol. 'But it's a chance. Some mighty interesting things have bin found under floor-boards.'

None of them realized how devastatingly interesting their own find was going to be.

11

Samsonville was about fifteen miles East of Trinity Valley. Once upon a time a gold-mine had been discovered there by an ex-circus performer, a strong man called 'Samson'. He had built the town and named it. When his gold-mine petered out he reverted to his old profession. He gathered around him old stars of the sawdust ring. He proclaimed Samsonville, 'The Mightiest Little Town in the World' and turned it into an amusement Mecca. A man could have a gamble there, or fill his eyes with the sight of freaks and all the pageantry of the circus. 'Samson' became very rich, he hired notorious gunmen to give shooting displays, ropers and riders and knife-throwers to show off their skill. If a man was famous in the West sooner or later he was hired by Samson.

Then this colourful character died and the heart went out of the business. The old circus-performers retired, the 'big men' became outsmarted or killed, or got out while the going was good. The get-rich-quick-boys, the gamblers and con-men and thugs and soaks — they all pulled out for pastures new. For a short time Samsonville was little more than another ghost town of the West. Then a bunch of settlers seeking land found these buildings ready-made for them and drove their stakes in there and farmed and run their stock. And Samsonville, though it never attained anything like its former glory, became a thriving little township once more.

Into the narrow Main Street of this place one hot dusty afternoon rode John Harding. He was weary and travel-stained, drooping in the saddle. His horse looked like he was on his last legs. The man straightened himself as he rode at a walking pace. He seemed to come alert in an instant; his head moved slowly. He looked around him with sharp, all-seeing eyes.

He observed the peeling-paint false fronts with the old signs, rain-washed but many of them still legible. The Golden Bowl Theatre had been converted into a huge livery-stables, there were carts at its double-doors, ploughs and other equipment strewed just inside its dim interior. Visitors still came sometimes to look at the old place and reconstruct its glory in their mind, so the townspeople left the ancient signs intact, they helped business. The old square high-walled amphitheatre, which had been the scene of some of Samson's mightiest shows, was still intact, and used for sales of stock and equipment, meetings and such-like.

The Blood and Bullets Saloon was still there, only under new management of course, and with very few girls and gamblers. The Two Feathers dance-hall across the street was now a big general stores, and most of the sporting houses and honky-tonks had been turned into either dwelling places or shops. The town had an aged mayor and a superanuated sheriff, both lapsing prematurely into senile decay for want of something to do.

The sheriff dozed in the sun and dreamt of past glories in Abilene, Santa Fe and Tombstone. The latter still hit the headlines from time to time. Just recently the 'West's fastest gun' had killed two men in its principal saloon. The sheriff sighed, a little complacently. Ah well, he was finished with all that kind of business. Famous gunmen didn't visit Samsonville anymore.

The sheriff dozed and nodded and, through half closed eyelids saw the tall dark-clothed stranger riding slowly down Main Street. There was something about the lean straight dark look of the man which struck a jangling chord in the sheriff's rusty memory. His mind seemed to creak like his chair as he leaned forward. Then he began to see pictures.

He saw a long bar, a man alone in its centre, a lean, dark young man. And another man advancing towards him, cat-like, Bo Sanderson his name had been. Bo Sanderson, the killer of Abilene. Bo Sanderson stopping, then blurring into action with a movement faster than the eye could see. And the young man at the bar moving slightly too, flame and smoke wreathing his hip. And, as the gun boomed Bo Sanderson falling, shot through the heart, his gun only half out of his holster.

Men had wanted to know the name of the cold-eyed younker who killed Bo Sanderson. They had learnt that it was John Harding. That was years ago, and now John Harding was a living legend. Many gunslicks had 'tried' the killer of Bo Sanderson, their gravestones were stepping stones in the career of the fastest gun in the West.

In his mind's eye the sheriff of Samsonville saw the face of the young man who stood against the bar that night in Abilene. And, looking up, he saw that face again in reality; a little older and tired, a little more remote, almost sad — but the same face.

The sheriff heaved himself to his feet. He felt young again as he rolled along the boardwalk. The man was steering his horse towards the livery stables when the soft voice behind him said: 'Howdy, John.'

He whirled, his hand at his belt, and the sheriff saw that bleak light in the bitter eyes which looked into his. Then recognition flashed into them, they softened. The man relaxed and held out his hand.

'It's Pete Larraby, isn't it?' he said.

'It's Pete Larraby all right.'

The old man gripped the extended hand. The sagging muscles of his face worked a little. The years seemed to fall from him, his body to straighten. The old eyes were bright, as if from unshed tears.

'It's good to see you again, John,' he said.

The other smiled and the sombre eyes were lit again. Of late such welcomes were becoming rarer. He waited for the inevitable question. It came — hesitantly, as if the old man was ashamed to voice it.

'You after anybody, John?'

Anywhere else the sting would have been there, the old bitterness, but the comically anxious look on the old man's face made Harding smile again.

'Not this time, ol' pard. Peace is all I want.'

The sheriff was young again, boisterous. 'You'll get it here, my boy. You'll get it.'

He ushered the man and his horse into the livery-stables. To the pudgy black youth who came out of the shadows he said: 'You take good care o' this cayuse, y'understand, Sam? It belongs to this gentleman an' he's a guest o' mine.'

The boy's face was swallowed by a huge row of gleaming teeth. 'Yassuh, mistuh sheriff,' he said. 'I'll give him mah own bunk.'

The old man aimed a swipe at his head, which the boy dodged with the ease of one accustomed to such sudden and aggressive movements. He took the horse.

The two men moved off. 'Stayin' long?' said the sheriff.

'Hadn't thought about it.'

'You're welcome to bunk with me as long as you like. I ain't got no kith or kin — there's plenty o' room in my place over the jail. It'll be peaceful enough for yuh — ain't had a prisoner since last Michaelmas.'

Harding made a grunting sound which might have been a chuckle. He said: 'It's mighty nice of yuh, Pete. I had expected to have to take a room in some godforsaken boardin' house or saloon. I don't want to put you out.'

The sheriff snorted. Such diffidence in this man rather surprised him. 'Plenty o' room,' he said. 'Glad to have yuh. Come on.'

By the following morning all Samsonville knew John Harding was in town. The black boy, Sam, had big ears and he used them to good advantage.

When Harding went to the Blood and Bullets to get a drink he was gawped at as if he was a performing elephant. 'There's one of 'em ol' Samson didn't get,' said an old-timer.

Harding had his drink and beat a speedy retreat back to the sheriff's place. These silent staring yokels gave him the creeps: he'd sooner face a bunch of sharp-shooters.

The sheriff had been out. When he returned he had news about the ruckus in Trinity Valley. 'Two men killed,' he said.

'Who were they?' asked Harding quickly.

'I dunno. You know how these things get around. I've had nothing official. Just rumours. By tomorrow it'll probably be six men killed — and still no names . . . Did you hit Trinity Valley on your wanderings, John?'

'I did.' Harding told him the whole of it.

When he had finished the old man's face was grave. 'D'yuh think this ruckus had anythin' to do with you?'

'Cain't see why. Mebbe I ought to go back there.' It seemed to the sheriff that Harding was unnecessarily worried.

The old man said: 'Forget it. Mebbe sump'n else will come through.'

His guest seemed preoccupied for the rest of the day, and after the evening meal said he would go for a browze. The old man decided to follow him but, because he had had a tiring day, fell asleep in his chair instead. And the Fates got on with their plans.

Perversity drove John Harding to the Blood and Bullets once more. If those yokels wanted to stare, well, let 'em! The place was packed. His entrance caused quite a stir. There was almost dead silence — then the chatter went on with redoubled vigour. People moved aside to let him through to the bar. Some looks were merely curious, others plainly resentful or unfriendly. The old bitterness welled up in Harding once more. He hadn't done anything to these people had he?

Maybe if he was to give them an exhibition of his draw, and shoot out the lights they'd be satisfied. Maybe that would give them a chance to run him out of town, to show him that they didn't want such as he in their stagnant little dump, to flaunt their civic pride. They were probably wondering why their sheriff had taken him in like a stray dog. Harding felt like laughing out loud at the thought. It was obvious that they did not know that their slow, affable old law-officer had ridden the owlhoot trail in his younger days.

Harding ordered a drink. He got it. Nobody stood too near him. He drank silently and alone. He was having his fourth when all heads turned towards the door again, and two strangers came in. Samsonville was having a surfeit of visitors.

These two were dirty, disreputable looking. They had evidently been riding hard. They were strangers to everybody in the place except the tall silent man at the bar. He recognized them

171

immediately. He had met them first tied together in the hands of a posse. They had had a pardner then. A big feller with his arm in a sling. John Harding had spent a night in jail with the three of them. He wondered how they had gotten out: Sheriff Hosell had seemed keen on keeping them. He wondered too, what had happened to the big fellow.

Malloy saw him first. He pretended not to, but his eyes gave him away. He nudged Jonesy and changed his course. They went to the end of the bar. Harding watched them through the mirror behind the bar. He saw Jonesy glance at him and then look quickly away. The two men put their heads together. Finally they seemed to come to a decision. They had a quick drink apiece then quitted the place.

John Harding was a sorely troubled man. He had to make a decision too. It did not take him long. He made it and acted upon it. He put down his empty glass and moved from the saloon, disregarding the glances thrown after him.

He strode quickly across a pool of light which spilled from the wide window, and halted in the deep shadows. He looked about him. There was no sign of the two men. A horseman passed slowly down the middle of the street. A walking man clattered along on the opposite board-walk.

Walking as quickly as possible, John Harding moved towards the livery-stables. He slackened his pace as he approached its doors. Then he stopped altogether as he heard voices. He backed into the narrow, black nick of an alley at the side.

He pressed his ear to the frame walls to hear the voices better. Then he heard a sound behind him, and as he whirled, reaching for his gun, he knew he had made a mistake. A blow on the side of his head knocked him to his knees in a morass of pain and giddiness. He knew then the voices did not belong to the two men. They were there before him.

'Get up, Mr Harding,' said a sneering voice. 'An' don't make any funny moves.'

He got up slowly, facing the two men, seeing the dull shine of the guns in their hands. They moved aside.

'Come past us,' said the one he knew to be called Stinger Malloy. 'Take it easy.'

He did as ordered, knowing there was nothing else to do, tense, waiting for an opening. Malloy's hand came out and took his gun. The lightness of his hip gave him a momentarily helpless feeling. This faded as he moved ahead of the two men. He had been right: they were running away from something. Had it something to do with the rumoured killings at Trinity Valley? In what way had his appearance thrown a hitch into their plans?

They moved out into a cleared space at the end of the alley. He turned. Malloy came forward, but the other man seemed uncertain. 'You were spyin' on us, Mr Harding,' said Malloy. 'What's your game?'

Harding did not answer. Malloy moved nearer. He was the cocky one, the vicious one. 'Answer me,' he said savagely. He poked the gun forward. Harding took a step backwards, banking on the assumption that the other man would not shoot if he could help it.

Malloy hid his savagery in rough sneering, trying not to get worked up. 'The great Mr John Harding. Skulking and spying. What do you want, uh? What are you goin' to do now, uh? You haven't got your gun: you're like a mangy dog with no teeth.' He moved forward again and this time Harding stood his ground and remained silent.

'Let's take him further out, Stinger,' said Jonesy nervously.

Malloy took no notice. He jerked his gun. 'By Jiminy, you'll speak 'fore I've finished with you,' he said. 'I'm asking questions. You answer 'em. What are you doin' here?'

'I could ask you the same one, pardner.'

'Oh, you *can* talk, uh? Why were you spyin' on us?'

This time Harding did not speak.

'Damn you!' said Malloy and moved forward, swinging the gun.

Harding's arm swung up, thudded into Malloy's. Malloy grunted. The gun went off.

Then the two men were grappling for it and Jonesy was dancing about, his gun ready, waiting to shoot. He got panicky. He could not see Harding: Malloy's body was in the way. A shot had been fired, an alarm given.

Malloy was saying, 'Get him, get him,' over and over again.

Jonesy darted forward. Malloy grunted in pain and staggered back towards him. Jonesy backed away again. He saw the gun in Harding's hand. His own finger was contracting on the trigger when the world seemed to explode about him. His body was filled with boiling water. He tried to call

Malloy's name, for Malloy to help him. He could not hear anything, could not see anything any more.

He died as Harding forced the cringing Malloy back up the alley.

As they reached the top a crowd burst upon them, surrounded them.

'Back,' snarled Harding. 'Back.'

He made an arc around him with the gun. His patience was exhausted. His face was gaunt, his mouth a thin stretched line. The people of Samsonville saw for a moment the killer upon whom they had spent so much speculation. They backed away as if there was a mad dog in their midst.

From behind them a voice said: 'What's goin' on here?' There were cries of 'the sheriff,' and information was thrown at him from all sides. Pete Larraby pushed his way through the mob.

'I want to clap this man in your jail, Pete,' said Harding. 'There's another up the alley. But I think he's dead.'

Shock rooted the sheriff to the spot.

But Harding was already moving forward, shoving Stinger Malloy in front of him with the barrel of his gun. Larraby came out his trance and, with a show of truculence, drew his gun and followed them. 'Make way there,' he said. 'Make way.'

Somebody shouted, 'Sheriff, there's a man lying back here.'

'All right, bring him up . . . Make way there.'

With the crowd still milling around them the cavalcade reached the office. They went inside and the sheriff shut the door in the people's faces.

A few minutes later a roar went up, and he had to open the door again to let in two men with their burden. Jonesy was dead all right. 'I don't want him,' said the old man. 'Making a mess all over the place. Take him to the undertaker's.'

The perplexed bearers backed out once more. What had come over old Pete?

The sheriff leaned his back against

the door and blew a little. Harding returned from locking Malloy in a cell. 'All right, John,' said Larraby. 'Start talkin'.'

While the crowd still murmured sullenly outside Harding started to talk. He was still talking after all the folks, for they were hardworking yokels, had gone home to their beds. The two men talked and smoked into the small hours and Larraby heard a tale.

A tale of fair fighting, of gunsmoke and glory — of snarling challenges, of more gunsmoke, of blood and death and the culminating bitterness and frustration. Of a man who kept riding, always riding, to escape his own destiny.

'I don't want to go around killing people, Pete,' said Harding desperately. 'I've killed enough. All I want now is peace. If I could find a little spread in some quiet corner I'd hang up my guns for good. If my damned public would let me go. The fastest gun in the West! Everywhere I go there's some fast-shootin' gent who aspires to take that

179

title. And we're back on the old merry-go-round. Look at Tombstone — there were two of them there — '

'I heard about that, John.'

'An' Trinity Valley — even in a little one-horse burg like that there was one. If he'd been tougher I might have had to've killed him.'

'Trinity Valley — ' said Pete Larraby. He paused then as if at loss for words.

'Have you had any more news, Pete?'

'No.'

'I've got friends back there — an' there's somep'n goin' on. I've an idea those two ginks I had the ruckus with tonight had something to do with. Last time I seen them they were in jail back there. Maybe they broke out. I'd like to go back there in the mornin', Pete — an' take that snake, who's in the cells now, back with me.'

The old man was silent for a bit. Then he said: 'It's a big thing you're askin', John.'

'I know, Pete. Mebbe you'd better sleep on it, uh?'

The old man nodded and rose. He said no more — except 'Goodnight.'

John Harding lay awake with his thoughts. It was very late when he dozed off into a half-sleep which was like a smoky haze peopled with phantoms, advancing on him from all sides, ringing him so that there was no escape. Somewhere among them, from time to time, he saw the anguished faces of those he loved, and they seemed to be calling him. Then, suddenly, someone had hold of him and he began to struggle. He heard Pete Larraby's voice and he remembered where he was.

'Come on, John. You'd better get goin' now before all the wise-acres get up.'

He rose. Dawn was filling the room with a smoky light which reminded him of his dream. The sheriff did not give him chance to speak.

'Your hoss is ready and waiting outside. An' one for the other man. Breakfast is ready.'

Then the old man was gone. John Harding put on his boots, buckled on his gun-belt. Breakfast was a silent meal.

Then the two men rose. They gripped hands.

'Thanks, Pete,' said Harding. 'I'll be back.'

A few moments later Pete Larraby stood on the boardwalk outside his office looking out along Main Street, watching the two horsemen ride into the blue haze of the early morning. One of them raised an arm above his head and waved. The sheriff waved back. The two horsemen disappeared over the smoky horizon. The old man sighed and returned slowly to his office.

12

The three men worked their way systematically to the back of the cabin, stripping off the boards and revealing the earth beneath, carpeted with the accumulated filth of years. Matchsticks, cigarette stubs, buttons. Unidentifiable rubbish, and a few coins.

Then at the back of the cabin Sol discovered a couple of boards which gave very little resistance to his crowbar. The ground beneath was scoured, fresh earth gleamed.

'Hey,' said the big Irishman. 'Looks like somebody's been messing around under here.'

He got down on his hands and knees. 'This hole goes right under the back of the cabin. There's a bundle or somethin'-or-other back there. Here — give me a hand with the rest of these boards.'

His brothers ran to his aid. Even the stolid Manny could not conceal his eagerness. They tore at the boards. 'Mebbe this is what we've been lookin' for,' said Pat. 'The fools. They might've known we'd think o' doin' this sooner or later.'

'The fools,' said Pat again.

Then the brothers fell silent as piece by piece the boards were moved. Sol had to use his crowbar once more, then they were against the wall of the cabin, but the hole continued underneath it.

'They must have shoved the stuff as far as they could get it,' said Pat, 'I guess I can reach it.'

He was the tallest of the three. He got down on his belly and reached a long arm into the aperture. He strained and grunted.

He began to withdraw his arm, then with a grunt of triumph brought a bulky bundle out into the light. 'Seems like there's still something else back there,' he said.

'Let's have a look at this,' said Sol

and pounced on it. It unrolled at his touch. Sol gave a sharp almost horrified exclamation.

'It's jest a bundle of clothes, nothing else. An' they've got blood on them.'

'Yeh,' said Manny. 'Yeah.'

Pat was down on his side again, looking into the aperture. When he rose his face was dirty, pale beneath the dirt.

'There's something else there. But it's half buried. I think we'd better go round back an' dig.'

They took floorboards with them and Sol's crowbar. With these improvized spades they dug. It did not take them long to unearth the bullet-riddled body. The dirty-white sack-like body of Big Carmody.

'God,' said Sol. 'This is somep'n we didn't expect. What's the meanin' of it?'

With mingled feelings they looked down at the pitiful sight. They had all seen violent death before, this one did not affect them unduly. They felt no pity for Carmody, only curiosity as to how, and why he had met such an end.

'Mebbe they had a row,' said Manny.

'Yeah,' said Pat. 'But there was more than just three of them to finish up with remember. How about that bunch who busted 'em outa the jail. Maybe they did it, all of 'em. More money to go round, if we're still assumin' they had the barbecue-takings. Mebbe they killed Carmody to shut his mouth. He allus did talk too much.'

'They shut his mouth all right,' said Sol. 'And they evidently didn't want anybody to know of his death. No chance of the buzzards gettin' at him here an' givin' the game away.'

'No use in us standin' here gabbin',' said Manny. 'We'd best take him back to town an' give him a decent burial, whether he deserves it or not. Take the clothes too. Then bring a gang of men out here to tear this place to pieces.'

'D'yuh still think the cash is around here?'

'Could be,' said Manny. 'Anyway,' he added with a sudden flash of wit, 'it'll find them bawling mavericks back in town somethin' to do to work their steam off.'

'Better put an armed guard on 'em, too,' said Sol sardonically. 'This is Silver Star property you know.' The limp white sack-like thing was covered up and tied to Manny's horse. The beast snorted and bridled at the smell of death, but was eventually calmed down. Manny got up behind Pat and the grim party set out for town.

★   ★   ★

During the absence of any law-officer in Trinity Valley, Judge Lynus spent a lot of time in the sheriff's office where he answered queries, doled out advice, and kept an eye on the populace. The old man had a new lease of life. Folks realized that, although he was a formidable old goat now, he must have been a real rip-snorter in his younger days.

With his black servant, Mose, he had blown into Trinity Valley nine years ago.

He had hired men and had a big house built for him on the hill. There he had opened up a practise as a lawyer. He did not get many cases but that did not seem to worry him. He seemed to have unlimited supplies of cash. People found him to be a just man, a cantankerous and unpredictable man, a fighter. He became known as 'Judge' and in this capacity had dispensed much justice of late. The usual rumours centred around him: he had had an unhappy love-affair; he had been struck off the rolls back East for some terrible misdemeanor. But nobody knew the truth about him — maybe he just liked the West.

Just after the judge arrived, the town had received another man of like nature, though different profession. This was John Mowbree, the printer, who brought his girl Sally, purchased the tumble-down old stores on Main Street, and turned it into a newspaper office.

There was not much known about

old John either, and he never talked about his past life. He and the judge were sort of friendly rivals, given to jousting at meetings, and occasionally 'cutting' each other on the street.

Now John Mowbree was dead, and Judge Lynus still reigned. He sat in state on a high chair in the window of the sheriff's office. When folks called to see him, Mose ushered them inside with the grave courtesy of an old-world butler.

From his porch the judge could see the whole of Main Street. He could see everybody who rode into town, who visited the stores or the Proud Valley Saloon. He eyed most of them with little interest in his heavy-lidded eyes.

It was late one afternoon when he saw the two riders come in slowly with heavy weariness in the look of them and their horses. The light was poor, and the judge leaned forward to get a better look, his eyes peering now, his seamed face suddenly taut.

The riders passed the saloon and

came on. The judge called his servant. 'Open the door,' he said.

The two men dismounted outside the office. Mose opened the door to them. The foremost one was unarmed. He walked with his head down. The one behind him had his hand on the butt of his gun. In the rear curious people were beginning to gather.

The judge held out his hand, 'Welcome back, Mr Harding,' he said. 'You've brought our prodigal with you I see. That takes care of two of them. Where is the other one?'

'He won't be coming,' said Harding. 'I'll tell yuh, Judge — but first of all have you got anything to drink?'

★ ★ ★

Doctor Billings said the sheriff's heart was getting stronger. Then finally he showed signs of returning consciousness, he began to mumble in delirium. He had had excellent care, the efforts of five people to bring him back to the land of the living. Mrs Murphy and Sally Mowbree took turns to nurse him, and the three brothers did all in their power to help. The little tubby doctor was in constant attendance. The whole town waited and hoped. Clay Hosell was a very popular lawman.

Sol Murphy sat by the bedside and listened to the mumblings. He bent nearer to the lean ashen face.

'Clay,' he whispered. 'Clay.'

The leaden eyes remained closed. The mumbling voice went on. At times it was shrill, then it died to a whisper. There were no words, no meaning.

Manny came up. 'Go downstairs an' get some chow, Sol,' he said. 'I'll watch him.'

Sol rose and lumbered down the stairs. His mother was sleeping in the back room. Sally had gone home, promising to return a little later. Sol found the kitchen empty, his supper warming on the hob. He calculated Pat must have gone with Sally. He took his chow across to the table, poured himself a cup of coffee, and set to.

Somebody rapped on the door. Sol was transfixed, a potato poised on his fork halfway to his mouth. Who could be calling this late? It could not be the doctor, he always came right in. Sol, ever cautious, reached for his gun. He held it under the table as he called, 'Come in.'

The door opened. The man who entered was tall, weary-looking, dark-garbed.

'John,' exclaimed Sol, springing to his feet.

Then something he saw in the man's face, his eyes, made him pause in his stride. The eyes were abysmal, and it seemed they were peering from a hard, lined mask.

'Who did it, Sol?' said John Harding.

Sol felt suddenly ashamed that he could not answer this question. He hung his head a little.

'I wished I knew,' he said. 'But we'll find out. Don't you worry, we'll find out . . . Sit down, John.'

The other man relaxed a little. As he let himself fall on to the old sofa against the wall his shoulders became bowed. The eyes that looked up into Sol's were unutterably weary. They had a lost, wondering look. Sol turned away, scared he might reveal the sudden pity he felt. Almost unconsciously he sat down to his meal once more.

'Carry on,' said John Harding. 'I'll rest.'

'Pour yourself some cawffee, John.'

'I don't need any.'

Sharp footsteps clattered outside. The latch clicked and the door opened. Sally Mowbree walked sharply into the room. Then she stopped dead as she saw the man opposite her. Pat, coming behind, almost bumped into her. His eyes widened, too.

'John,' the girl said huskily. 'John.'

'Hallo, Sally,' he said. 'Long time no see.'

The girl seemed suddenly oblivious of everybody else in the room. She went over to the man and dropped on one knee in front of him. She took both his hands in hers. He looked down at her. The mask had dropped, he looked suddenly ten years younger. His lips moved as if searching for words, and finding the task difficult.

'John,' the girl said again. 'I thought I'd have seen you before. I thought you'd come. John, Dad — '

He interrupted her quickly. 'I know, Sally, I know. I didn't come the last time — you didn't come — I thought Dad was still that way.'

'Pride,' said the girl in a half-choked voice. 'Pride with both of you. He was waiting for you to come, John. He wanted you to come.'

'I didn't know, Sally,' said the man softly. 'I didn't know.'

Pat Murphy shut the door. 'What — ?' he said. Then he stopped. He looked bewildered, a little truculent.

The girl rose, half-turned. 'Pat,' she said. 'This is my brother, John. Although he calls himself Harding his proper name is Mowbree.'

'I didn't want to bring disgrace on the family name,' said the man. There was a trace of the old bitterness in his voice. 'Now it's too late. I — '

The girl put her hand on his arm, she said quickly, 'Pat.'

Pat came forward. 'John,' went on Sally. 'This is Pat Murphy. We're going to be married.'

'We've met,' said John Harding. Something resembling a smile crossed his face. 'How are you, cowboy?' He stretched out his hand.

Pat took it. He grinned. 'I'm fine,' he said.

'Congratulations.'

'Thanks.'

All three of them sat down. But in a second Sally jumped up again.

'How's the sheriff?' she said.

'Still mumbling,' said Sol through a mouthful of food. 'But he's livin', praise the saints. I guess he'll soon be kicking an' cursing like he useter. Manny's up there.'

'I'll go up,' said Sally. She looked

around at the three men. Their faces were hard. They were waiting for her to go so that they could talk. She was not needed there any more.

'I'll send Manny down,' she said as she went up the stairs.

The three men were silent until Manny came and Harding had greeted him. Then Sol said: 'Where did you hear about it, John?'

'In Samsonville. I met a couple of galoots there, too, who tried to jump me. One of 'em's dead. I brought the other one back with me.'

He told them the full story. The three men told him their own and Sol said: 'Looks like Stinger Malloy's our only link now then. He knows. But will he talk?'

John Harding rose. 'If he won't there are ways and means of making him do so.'

The three men looked at him. The younger one shuddered at something he saw in those cold eyes. Here was a man who would stop at nothing. Nothing at all. And, strangely enough, Pat could understand him and feel for him.

'How about the judge?' said Sol. 'He might be awkward.'

'We'll cross that bridge when we come to it,' said John Harding.

He took a few paces across the room. 'You folks ready?'

'Now?'

'Now.'

'I'll tell Sally we're going out,' said Pat. He went up the stairs.

The other three stood by the door and waited for him. When he returned his face was set, his eyes hooded.

'Let's go,' he said.

'All I want is a little moral support,' said John Harding sardonically, and in that moment Pat did not like him.

13

It was late. The street in front of the jail was deserted. All the night-life of Trinity Valley was centred around the Proud Valley Saloon and kindred places.

In his cell Stinger Malloy heard the tramp of boots on the boardwalk. There was something rather ominous about the steady resounding thud-thud. Stinger was apprehensive because he had been left in peace so long. The only human he had seen since he was clapped in the cell was the negro man who brought him chow, and was as silent and impassive as a drug-store Indian.

For all the sound that came from out front, Stinger might have been sealed in a cave in the middle of an empty desert. Then came the thud of feet, purposeful, ominous. They stopped outside the jail, and he heard the door open and the rumble of voices.

He tried to listen to what was being said but the words were indistinguishable. He tried to cull some information from the sound of the voices. They went on and on with an even tremor, soulless. Then he heard the door of the cell-block open. They were coming for him. He had been left alone at the mercy of a lynch-party. He might have known that killer, Harding, and that old man and his devil of a negro servant, were cooking up something like that.

But it was only a single pair of heels that clattered in the passage. And one man only stopped outside the cell-door. Stinger saw that it was the killer, Harding, who looked at him through the bars and said nothing. Stinger went cold all over. Was this the end? To be shot like a dog in a corner through the bars of a cage? Was this to be his finish? His voice was high as he said: 'What do you want?'

The other man still did not answer.

His face was in the shadows. It was barred and hard, the eyes like black sockets.

Then his hand moved from behind his back and Stinger saw the keys as they were inserted in the lock. The door swung open and John Harding came in. Only then did Stinger realize that he was not wearing his gun-belt and new hope surged through him. He tensed. What was this game? What was this fancy gunman — minus a gun — trying to pull? He rose.

'What do you want?' he said again.

The other man did not reply. He stood there looking at Stinger, and Stinger found it difficult to meet his eyes.

He became truculent and, as if reading the other man's mind, said: 'You won't get nothin' outa me, Harding.'

The other man spoke at last. 'Won't I?' he said. There was no trace of any feeling whatsoever in his voice.

'Is there anything there at all to come

out of you, friend?' said the voice.

Stinger was nonplussed by this oblique question. He did not say anything. He shifted his feet. His eyes too. This man had the keys in his belt. And he was unarmed.

Leastways, he looked like he was unarmed. Stinger, a sly, vicious man himself, was very leary. Maybe the galoot had a derringer tucked away somewhere. Maybe he was just waiting for Stinger to make a move so that he would have a chance to plug him. Maybe it was all a put-up job between this killer and that snarling old jackass in the office. The old gag: shooting the prisoner in the act of escaping.

'Don't just stand there,' he said. 'What are you after?' He tried to make his voice sound tough, level, but he could not keep that strained high note out of it. This man gave him the creeps.

Harding said softly, as if to himself: 'If there's anythin' to come out of you I guess it'll come out sooner or later.'

'Don't talk in riddles,' said Stinger in

his high voice. 'I ain't keen to have conversation with you. An' whether you're John Harding or Bronco Bill you don't scare me.'

'A funny man,' said John Harding. 'Talk some more, funny man. Tell me what you know. All of it. Maybe we could make a deal, funny man.'

'Go to hell,' said Stinger. He was becoming heartened. He still didn't know what the game was, but the notorious gunman hadn't yet made any aggressive movements.

Maybe he just wanted to speil, to show off his wits. He wasn't so smart!

'Go to hell, Mr Harding,' said Stinger, driving his point home. 'For you — I don't know anythin'.'

The unemotional voice said: 'You don't know who killed the man at the barbecue, and got the money, who raided the jail and got you out, and killed John Mowbree and the deputy. You don't know any of that?'

'I don't know nothin'.' Stinger's mouth remained fixed open; his other smart sayings died in his throat as Harding's fist flashed out and connected with his ear.

It seemed to drive that member into his very brain, splitting his head wide open. He went back on to his bunk, jarring his elbow hard against the wall. He throbbed with pain. When the haze cleared a little John Harding was still standing there. Stinger launched himself at the tall form.

His fist connected with Harding's shoulder. The bars of the door rattled as Harding crashed back upon them. Vicious triumph glowed in Stinger and he bored in, throwing more blows.

If he could get hold of those keys!

He was throwing punches at Harding, when suddenly Harding was not there any more. Stinger squealed in pain as his fist crashed against the iron bars of the cage. Too late he realized he was being hazed. As he spun another punch landed on his already damaged ear. His shoulder crashed into the door, which held him up. Two more agonizing blows bit into his face. He swayed forward, striking out blindly.

He doubled up as another fist sank into his midriff. Then he was straightened up again by a blow on the chin. In the midst of his pain was the blinding realization that he was being cut to ribbons. He must do something against this man! He swung a foot, savagely — felt it connect.

John Harding was swaying. Mad with pain and rage Stinger rushed at him blindly. Next moment they were rolling together on the floor of the cell.

Stinger bit and scratched and kicked, crazy to hold on to his advantage, to get the better of this man, to get those keys. He had his hand on them, tried to pull them away from the belt. Then Harding hit him again, a terrific blow clean between the eyes.

Stinger lay on his back on the floor of the cell and he was alone. The ceiling was receding far far away from him. He was trying to rise up towards it. Then hands were grabbing him and he didn't want to be hurt again and he tried to say so. And a voice said: 'Talk then. Talk!'

Things became clearer again. Stinger saw the dark hated face of Harding looking down into his. A surge of hope filled the prisoner again, and hate that almost choked him. He clawed upwards at the face. Then the face was moving away from him and he was being hauled to his feet. A cruel hand was at his throat and a balled fist hit him again and again. Not with stunning force but with almost scientific finesse. He tried to pull his head away from it, but the hand at his throat held him, the thumb dug cruelly into his Adam's apple. Everything spun around him, a mist whirled, shot with red lights. All was pain.

The sharp blows ceased to fall, and a hand was pushed under his chin. He was sent spinning until he crashed against the wall on to his bunk.

The haze lightened a little and through it the tall dark form advanced again. The voice said, 'Talk will you, or, I'll tear you to ribbons.'

Stinger found that he could not speak. He croaked and some devil inside of him, something, it seemed, over which he had no control, made him shake his head. Then his face was slapped — right, left — right, left. And with each blow his head cracked against the wall and knives jabbed through his temples, his eyeballs, his nose and his jaw. He tried to cover up with his hands, and a fist smashed into his stomach. He gulped, and his hands dropped as he came forward. Then a blow in his face straightened him up again and his head hit the wall once more.

He kicked out feebly and the same thing happened again: a sickening blow in the stomach then one in the face to straighten him up. Then a hand held him up as he lolled and the voice said: 'Will you talk? Will you?'

Stinger yammered and croaked. Then, like a flood suddenly released, the words spilled out in a choking scream.

'Yes, I'll talk! Leave me alone! I'll talk I tell yuh — I'll talk!'

* * *

John Harding came back into the office. 'He spilled it all,' he said. 'I've left some for the hangman.'

He sat down and rested his hands on his knees. The other men noticed that those hands were trembling.

'Well?' said Judge Lynus harshly.

'Him and Jonesy raided the barbecue. He said it was Jonesy who killed Luke Sands. I have my doubts about that — it's all I could get out of him on that score.'

'The crime was shared between them anyway,' said the old man tersely. 'He'll hang all right.'

'The crime was engineered by Jasper Hart. The men took their actual orders — and details of the plan — from Brad Simmons but, of course, both those jaspers were at the barbecue to throw suspicion off themselves. Nobody else at the Silver Star knew about the job — except Carmody, of course: he was look-out at the line-out, covering-up for Malloy and Jonesy in case anybody ambled along while they were doing the job. Malloy went right back to the cabin, Jonesy rode to the ranch and stashed the money — in the ranch-house. He had just come back from there when you boys jumped.'

'He took a big risk,' said Pat Murphy.

'It was a bold plan. Hart's on his uppers — his place is mortgaged to the hilt. Apart from that, he hates the settlers like pizen — he hates every-body. This was his way of getting his revenge — and enriching himself at the same time.'

'You boys threw a wrench in the works when you picked up those three skunks. They had to be gotten loose before one of 'em talked. The real danger was Carmody. If the other two talked they would only be putting their own necks in the noose. But Carmody had taken no active part in the job, hadn't done any killing. He might sing to save himself.

'So Brad Simmons — who must be a reg'lar young hellion — worked the Silver Star boys into a lather by telling 'em that the capture of their three pardners was a put-up job by the settlers, that they were innocent of any crime, but they'd be scragged by a lynch-party if they weren't gotten out of jail pronto. Quite naturally, the boys believed every word of it and that night Simmons led a picked bunch of them on the raid. It was Simmons, the leader, who killed Lew Connors and my father, and wounded the sheriff — '

Towards the end Harding's voice went husky. He paused, his head sunk.

'Simmons,' said Sol softly. 'That fancy panty-waisted buzzard all along.'

Harding looked up. 'Simmons,' he echoed. 'Yes — He's mine you understand — all of yuh. He's mine.'

'Sure, John.'

'How about Carmody?' said Pat.

When Harding spoke again his voice was cold, level — normal once more.

'Wal, Simmons gave the three men part of the stolen money and told them to hit the trail, to lie low till the heat had blown off. Carmody was sick and he didn't want to run. Seeing as he'd taken no actual part in the killings he didn't see why he should run. He thought the boss should protect him. He got ugly. Simmons killed him, filled him full o' lead, and they buried him where you found him later ... ' Harding paused, spread his hands. 'That's it,' he said.

The men began to rise, there was purpose in all their eyes. It only needed one of them to voice it. They were grim, ready for action, and, as one man, they whirled as sharp footsteps clattered on the boardwalk outside. The footsteps stopped. The door was rapped, then immediately flung open. Sally Mowbree came in. She said, huskily, breathlessly: 'The sheriff's all right: He's talking. He said the raiders must have been Silver Star men. Before he lost consciousness he heard the leader call two names. 'Bull', and, 'Jodey'.' Bull Rawsthorne and Jodey Canning. Both Silver Star men. 'He said the leader's voice sounded very familiar too. It sounded like Brad Simmons . . . '

'We know all that now, Sally,' said John Harding softly. 'Stinger Malloy talked.'

'Did he?' said the girl. She looked at her brother. At that moment he seemed like a stranger to her. Not the happy-go-lucky brother she had known and loved, but the cold-hearted, merciless gunman of legend. She looked from one to the other of the rest of the men. A little quiver ran through her slight, supple frame.

'Brad Simmons killed father an' Lew Connors an' shot the sheriff,' said John Harding.

'Brad Simmons,' echoed the girl. She shuddered. 'And to think I hobnobbed with him. I even liked him for a time.'

'Forget it, honey,' said Pat softly.

The girl took a step towards him, then halted. She saw the purpose in his face, in all their faces. She knew she could not do anything more there. Everything else that had to be done was men's work — the women's work would maybe come later. The thought was chilling. Her eyes were dark, full, as she looked again at Pat. 'I guess I'll go back to the sheriff,' she said.

'Tell him we'll be down later,' said Pat. '*Chiquita*.'

The caressing endearment floated after her as she closed the door. None of the men spoke until her footsteps faded away.

'You've got a jewel in that gel,' said the phlegmatic Manny suddenly.

'Yeah,' said Pat. 'Yeah.' He was the lover no more; he was the fighter now — raring to go.

It was Sol who voiced his younger brother's thoughts, all their thoughts. He was looking at the judge as he said: 'The only thing we can do now is get a posse of picked men together, and ride on the Silver Star.'

The old man took it very coolly. 'I know there isn't nothing else to do,' he said. He turned to his negro servant, who had stood silently in the background. 'Mose, fetch my pistols.'

The negro's graven face broke into a huge grin. 'Yes, suh,' he said. 'I'll be back in a shake.' He went.

The other men had hardly gotten over their surprise at the old man's sudden decision before the servant had returned. He tendered a large leather case. He patted his own belt where his black coat flew open. A huge Colt .45 reposed there.

'Good boy,' said the judge.

He opened the case, revealing a pair of long-barrelled, silver-plated duelling pistols reposing in velvet, a box of shells in the smaller compartment beside them. The old man took out a gun and weighed it in his hand. A silver plaque gleamed in the bottom of the box. The judge indicated it.

'Finest shot in the Officer's Corps,' he said absently.

As the men watched him silently he began to load the guns. Mose crossed the room and stood attentively beside him. His body was erect, his arm straight, his fingers to the red-piped sides of his trousers. His face was grave.

The two men were alone in a little world of their own, the old soldier handling his guns with loving care, his batman ready there to obey his slightest wish.

'We'll go round up the boys,' said Sol Murphy softly.

14

The old warrior rode at the head of his troop in the early morning light. As they advanced on the ranch-buildings he ordered them to spread out, and the two flanking parties to move on a little faster. The settlers, old Indian fighters many of them, lay flat over the saddles of their horses, so that only their legs would be seen from the ranch-house. They held their guns ready, their hands against the horses' necks.

Judge Lynus sat erect in the saddle, brought his arm over and forward in a sweeping motion, and set spurs to his big bay horse. The magnificent beast, tired of being hitched between the shafts of a carriage, smelling battle and action once more, bounded forward like a spring released.

Rifles glinted in the windows of the Silver Star ranch-buildings. Word of the capture of Stinger Malloy had evidently reached them. They had been half-expecting an attack. They waited till the strung-out charging settlers were in range then opened fire.

Jenky, the ancient keeper of the feed-barn was the first to topple from the saddle. He was dead before he hit the ground. He had insisted on coming, his blood had been re-fired by a promise of action, the return of glory. He had his glory — maybe he was content in that split second between the numbness after the shot hit him and the time he died.

Another man rolled on the ground. He rose, cursing, and with one blood-streaming arm hanging at his side, caught his horse with the other and vaulted into the saddle. Judge Lynus's hat was whisked from his head. He did not turn a hair. He waved his long barrelled pistol and boomed, 'Spread out!'

The settlers were already doing so. There had been a brief moment of

216

almost-panic by those men who were not used to this kind of fighting, but their casualties were light. No more serious ones apart from Jenky. They spread out wider and, riding Indian-fashion, began to make flanking movements on the long log bunk-house from whence the hottest fire had come. They opened up themselves.

The firing from the other side was now more spasmodic, they were trying to pick off their men. The settlers were moving fast. A horse screamed with pain and buckled at the knees, throwing its rider over its head. The man rose, limped towards the horse. The beast lay still. The man looked around him. He fell flat on his stomach. Bullets whistled above him. His gun out, he retaliated. One of his pardners rode beside him, stopped his horse prancing. The rider held out his hand. The other man took it as he rose from the ground. He vaulted up behind the rider who turned his horse's head. A few ineffectual shots winged after them as they sped out of harm's way.

Another rider whose horse was shot from under him was not so lucky. The beast had stopped a bullet in the fleshy part of his rump and writhed on the ground in agony. The man, his ankle twisted, crawled towards the beast, put his gun to its head and pulled the trigger.

The man rose and, drawing another gun, blazed away at the windows of the bunk-house as he backed swiftly. There was no one on hand to succour him. It seemed like he would make it. He was turning to run when he paused in his stride, his body half-twisting. He was transfixed there for a moment, then his body arched backwards and he fell in a crumpled heap. Another settler rode furiously to his aid, looked down at the still figure, pursed his lips in sudden sadness, and charged onwards.

The settlers were moving in now. They were around the back of the place too. Three cowhands, trying to escape that way, had been shot down. The firing from the bunk house had a spasmodic desperate sound about it. A portion of the full strength were still out on the range, guarding the cattle. They had orders to ride in at the first sounds of trouble. There was no sign of hide nor hair of any of them. They had probably lit out for another state! Who could blame them? The trapped men cursed their boss's avariciousness and wished they were well out of this too.

'I vote we give in,' said one huge ranny. 'Ain't no use in sticking our necks out for that skunk in the ranch-house.'

'He probably ain't in the ranch-house now. He probably high-tailed with his fancy woman — an' Simmons too — an' left us to hold the baby.'

In this the man who spoke was not strictly correct. By arrangements beforehand the Murphy brothers and John Harding had advanced on the ranch-house.

They were just in time to prevent Hart, his wife, and the blond-headed ramrod from making a break. They were driven back inside by a hail of shots.

'It's a pity that female's there,' said Sol.

'Don't let that stop yuh,' said John Harding in that bitter sardonic voice of his.

The four men dismounted from their horses. They ran for the shelter of outhouses as the men opened up viciously from inside the ranch-house.

'That place's built like a fort,' said John Harding. 'They're well covered.'

'They're trapped too,' said Sol. 'If they go out the front way they'll be shot down like clay pigeons. If they want to come out they've gotta come this way. An' I'm damn' sure they won't get past us.'

Old Judge Lynus seemed to bear a charmed life. He rallied his men and led them once more in a charge. From the back of the bunk-house came the crackle of firing from the others of the main party who were stopping any outlets that way.

Mose, the faithful negro man, rode beside the old soldier and a little way behind him. The judge heard him grunt suddenly and he turned in the saddle. Mose's eyes were wide, the whites showing; his face was puckered in agony.

The old man whirled his horse with a jerk of the reins. He caught his old servant as he fell forward. Another man rode up. Together they dismounted and laid Mose on the ground. His breast was already a mass of blood. He opened his eyes again and tried to say something. All he could manage was a harsh croak.

'Mose,' said the old judge. 'Mose.' The old soldier, his mask broken, was beside himself with anguish. He caught hold of his old friend's hands. He held them tightly, desperately. There was a faint smile on Mose's ebony face as he died.

The judge rose. He was the coldly-calculating leader once more.

'Take him back,' he said.

Then he remounted and, brandishing his pistol, rode forward with the rest of his men. There was naked savagery in his old eyes.

'Keep going!' he shouted. 'Keep going. We'll finish 'em this time.'

His voice was resounding, but even so it was doubtful whether anybody heard him. The settlers were whooping and shrieking madly as they charged, Indian-fashion. With dramatic suddenness a white flag was thrust through one of the bunk-house windows and waved wildly.

'Don't stop riding,' boomed the judge, suspecting a trick. 'Pull off and circle. Take cover.'

As his men spread out, moved to the sides of the bunk-house, or sought cover, he raised his voice once more: 'You men in there — throw your guns through the windows.'

There was a lull, a sudden silence.

Then the guns began to come through the windows and thud to the earth. Finally a voice bawled: 'That's the lot. We're finished.'

'No funny movements or we'll shoot you down like dogs,' boomed the judge. 'All of you come out the front with your hands above your heads.' He turned to one of his men. 'Ride around back and tell those men there to move on through an' see if there's anybody skulking.'

The man went. As he did so the bunk-house door opened and the beaten Silver Star men began to file out with their hands elevated.

★   ★   ★

The sudden silence was like a pall over everything. The crackle of gunfire behind the ranch-house was a subdued echo. Then that stopped too.

Sol Murphy said: 'Looks like they've given up there.'

He put his head out to have a look,

then ducked as a slug from the ranch-house almost took his nose off.

He turned and discovered his brother Pat grinning at him.

'Funny ain't it?' said Sol.

'Yeah, very funny. Whoever fired that shot must've taken you for a turkey.'

Sol scowled. 'Remind me to give you a good lacin' as soon as we get out o' this.'

'I'll remind yuh, you big turkey,' said Pat. 'I'll feather yuh an' truss you up for Christmas.'

'Cut it out you two,' said Manny parrot-like. It was his usual plea.

With a final half-humorous glare at each other Pat and Sol subsided. They watched the back of the ranch-house. Silent now, dead.

The four men crouched in a little feed-barn and stable. Behind them three horses champed. They belonged to the house, for the four horses belonging to the attackers were round back of the outhouses out of harm's way.

The three horses in the stable were bridled and saddled, had water-bottles and bedrolls attached to them. The two conspirators and the woman had evidently been ready for a quick getaway if need be — but had left it a little too late. They had been burdened by cases as they descended the steps, before they were driven back into the house by the attackers' fire. Once more it seemed, their tendency to grab all they could, to leave nothing of real value behind, had proved their undoing.

John Harding rose to his feet and stood in the shadows, just in cover of the stable-door. 'I'll give 'em a hail,' he said.

He raised his voice and shouted, 'Hart — Simmons — the place is surrounded — your men have given in. You haven't got a chance. If you don't come out purty soon we'll give the settlers the go-ahead to set the place on fire.'

He shut up. They waited. Everybody was silent. Maybe they were thinking of the woman in there. She was a fast, loathsome, painted woman from the East, but she was female flesh, and these rather quixotic Westerners did not want to harm her if they could help it. The thought did not enter their heads that maybe she, indirectly, was to blame for the tragedies of Trinity Valley, her extravagance and lust had driven her husband finally into half-crazy pillage and murder. There was Simmons too — maybe he was to blame as much as any of them. He was evidently a cold-blooded murderer, a ravening wolf in sheep's clothing who had at last shown his fangs.

Two of the settlers came running around the back of the ranch-house.

'Get back,' bawled Pat Murphy. 'Back.'

As he yelled a gun boomed from the ranch-house. One man clutched his arm and spun on his heels. They both got back out of harm's way.

'Get in cover,' bawled Pat. 'Surround the place.'

There was silence except for the subdued murmur of voices. Then there was the sound of Judge Lynus's ringing voice. The men in the stable could not hear what he said, but they knew the settlers were taking up positions.

John Harding raised his voice again. 'You ain't got much longer, you damn fools. You'd better come out with your hands up.'

The answering cry came then: high, harsh, desperate.

'We're coming out. Don't shoot. We're coming out.' It was Jasper Hart's voice.

Two guns came through the window, clattered on to the boards of the veranda. The back door opened.

Jasper Hart and his wife came out. He was supporting her with his hand beneath her elbow. She was hatless, her hennaed hair in disarray around her painted face. She tottered a little as she walked as if her legs could not support the weight of her body. Jasper Hart walked slowly. He seemed to be very gentle with her. His spare figure was erect in his black broadcloth. He was hatless, but he wore riding-boots, on the heels of which spurs glittered.

The man and his wife were both dressed for a trip, a trip which had suddenly been cancelled. They came slowly down the steps, he with his head erect, his narrow pale face pinched and set; she with her head downcast. He held one arm up in the air.

'Where's the other one?' said Pat Murphy.

He started forward. Sol grabbed his arm, holding him. Even as Pat turned and looked into his brother's face two shots rang out from the ranch-house.

The man and the woman fell together, crumpling up like two puppets whose strings had been suddenly cut. Horror transfixed the men in the stables for a moment. Then, cursing horribly, savagely, Pat Murphy darted forward. Sol grabbed for him again and missed. Pat reached the door. A shot boomed in the ranch-house once more.

Pat fell backwards silently. Sol caught him, his eyes staring, anxious.

Pat clutched his upper arm; blood streamed through his fingers.

'All right,' he said. 'I guess I asked for that.'

Settlers began to move into view again.

'Get back!' bawled John Harding.

Shots crackled from the ranch-house once more. A man cried out and fell. He dragged himself along on the ground, his hand pressed to his thigh. One of his pardners ran out to help him. They reached cover.

There was a sudden flurry of movement at the side of the stables. The men tensed, then relaxed as Judge Lynus dived through the door. Bullets thudded into the wood, a chip stung the old man's cheek, making it bleed.

'You take some awful chances, you old goat,' said Pat, very disrespectfully.

The judge smiled tiredly. Then he said: 'Mose is dead.' The poignancy of the single sentence made the other four men bow their heads for a moment.

'Looks like Simmons means to hang on there an' get as many of us as he can before we get him,' said Manny, facing facts as always.

'Mebbe I can get him out,' said John Harding softly. 'He's a very vain man. I used to be that way myself.'

The others looked at him in puzzlement. He rose to his feet and shouted, 'Hold your fire, everybody.'

'Let's burn him out,' shouted an irate settler.

'Be quiet!' bawled Harding. 'Simmons, can you hear me? This is John Harding talking.'

'I hear yuh.'

'All right, I'm giving you a sporting chance. You fancy yourself as a slick gunny don't you? Maybe you'd like to be the fastest gun in the West . . . Are yuh listening?'

'I'm listening, Harding.'

'Walk out with your gun sheathed, your hands by your side. I'll meet you halfway, give you an even break

— which is more than you deserve. If you kill me you'll be given a chance to run for it. D'you hear me, everybody? If he kills me he'll be given a chance to run for it, a chance to get clear altogether. I've lost more than any of you, he killed my father. I'll stand by that.'

His voice ceased. The old judge pursed his lips but said nothing. There was dead silence, no dissenting voice.

'You've got your chance, Simmons. Come on out.' Harding's voice died away into a subdued echo. Again there was silence.

The back door of the ranch-house opened and Brad Simmons came out. He stood on the veranda for a second with his hands hanging by his side. Then he began to descend the steps.

He reached the ground, his hands swinging loosely as he advanced. His blond hair glinted in the morning sunshine. His handsome face was set, sardonic, but his eyes shifted as he looked around him. He stepped daintily around the bodies of the two people he had murdered.

His eyes became focused as John Harding came out of the stables and strode to meet him. He stopped walking then. Although his body did not seem to bend, he gave the effect of crouching, and his fingers were clawed.

John Harding kept on walking, advancing slowly. His face was like a mask; his eyes seemed to be a little dilated. They were fixed on Simmons's face, on *his* eyes.

Simmons's eyes were wide, too, then they flickered a little as he went for his gun. Then they widened more so as, even as his fingers contracted, he knew he had failed. Terror paralysed his brain.

Harding had hardly seemed to pause in his stride, as if his draw was part of his walk. Simmons fell to his knees as the slug hit him in the chest. The boom of the gun awakened echoes, the blue smoke drifted. Simmons did not hear this, did not see anything. He fell on his face in the dust. His gun was still in his holster; his fingers clutched at the ground like dead claws. He lay still.

★　★　★

Sally Mowbree ran from the print-shop as the cavalcade came down the street. She ran to Pat, with John Harding beside him.

'*Honey*, you're hurt!'

'Just a scratch, *chiquita*. It'll be all right for the wedding . . . I've brought the best man back with me.'

He grinned and indicated Harding.

A slow smile crossed the other man's face. He seemed at loss for words. His eyes glowed as he looked down at his sister.

Pat said: 'He's staying here. He's gonna have three big Irish brothers-in-law to stop tough kids from picking on him.'

A grunting chuckle broke from Harding's lips. He took off his gun-belt and handed it down to his sister.

'Hang this up somewhere for me, Sally,' he said.

THE END